The Black Devil 3 & the Revenge of Desolation

"The black devil 3 is fully action-packed from start to finish, with plenty of emotion, plot twists and a fantastic story line that would leave you wanting more".

"The only book that makes you feel like you're actually watching a movie while reading."

" The Black Devil 3 is an extremely simple and fun book to read. It is not your typical complicated and boring book. It is uniquely written, and it reads like a thrilling comic book and a graphic novel."

"The Black Devil 3 is the next generation of superhero entertainment."

"Jaw-dropping entertainment that will leave you speechless and amazed guaranteed."

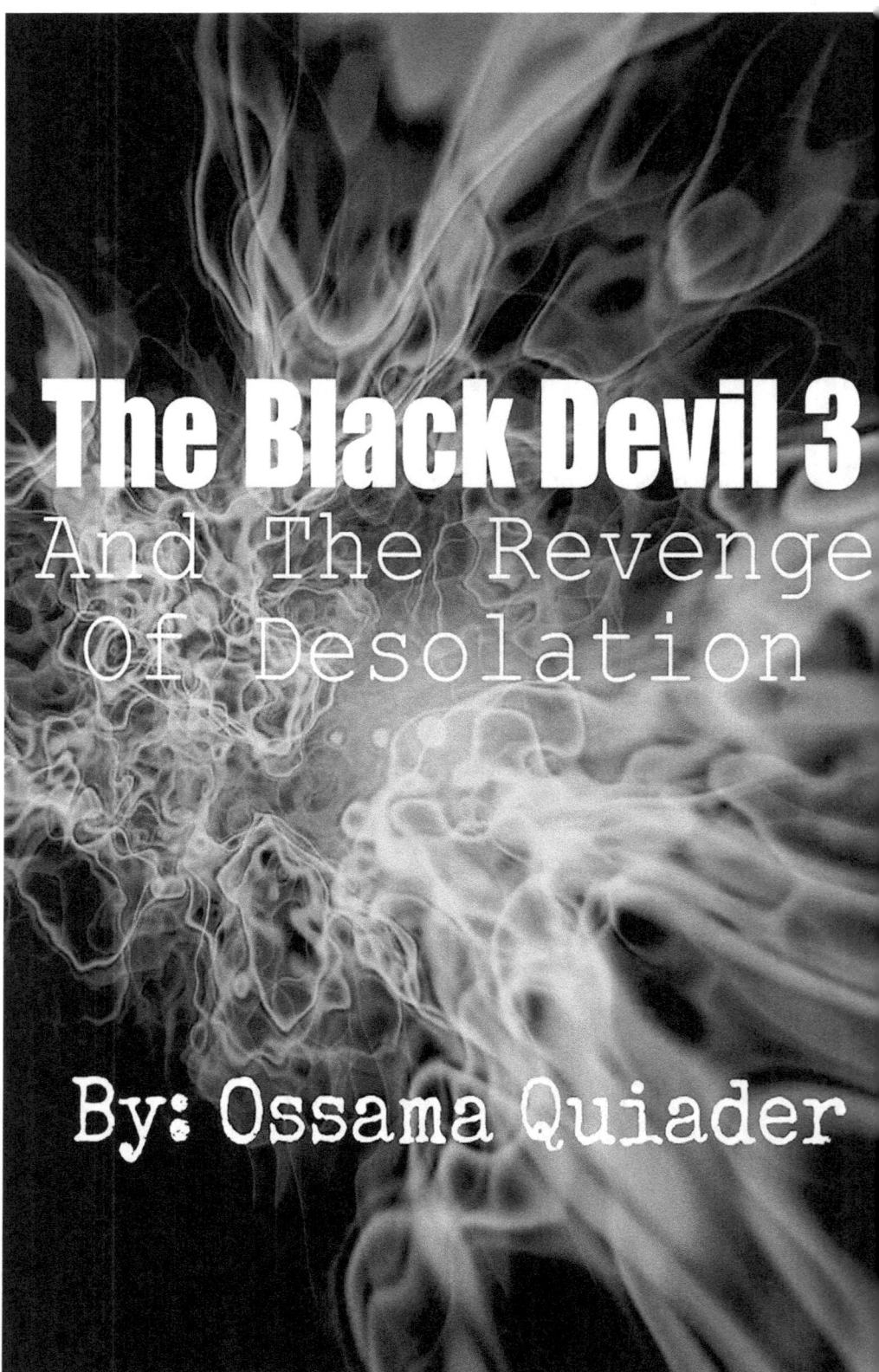

The Black Devil 3
And The Revenge Of Desolation

By: Ossama Quiader

Before reading go to YouTube and play these soundtracks while reading this book for an out-of-this world experience; these soundtracks will improve your reading experience by 80%:

1. Starvation by Thomas Bergersen

2. Interstellar No Time For Caution (Extended)

3. Man of Steel OST Mix "Zod Suite"

4. Hans Zimmer - Arcade [Extended]

5. Man of Steel OST Flight extended

6. The Dark Knight Trilogy theme

7. Deshi Basara OST Mix Extended Version

8. 11. The Dark Knight Rises (2012) Rise Theme (Soundtrack OST)

9. The Dark Knight Rises (main theme)

10. The Dark Knight Rises - Imagine the Fire

11. The Fountain Soundtrack - Death is The Road to Awe by Clint Mansell

You may not use any of my material; no part of this work may be reproduced stored in a retrieval system or transmitted in any form or by any means, electronic, mechanical, photocopying, recording, or otherwise without permission of the publisher, owner and founder of the Electrolyte Entertainment and Electrolyte Comics brand, Mr. Ossama Quiader. You may, however, share the front and back cover of my current book on all social media platforms such as Facebook, Twitter, Instagram, etc., but please remember to give me credit. Thank you.

Paperback ISBN: 9780994484208

For any business inquiries or feedback please contact me by email or contact number:

My email: quiader22@yahoo.com.au
Home phone: 97085717
Mobile phone: 0406 012 625
I live in Sydney, Australia.

THE BLACK DEVIL 3 AND THE REVENGE OF DESOLATION

The Black Devil 3

And The Revenge Of
Desolation.

The Black Devil 3

&The Revenge Of Desolation

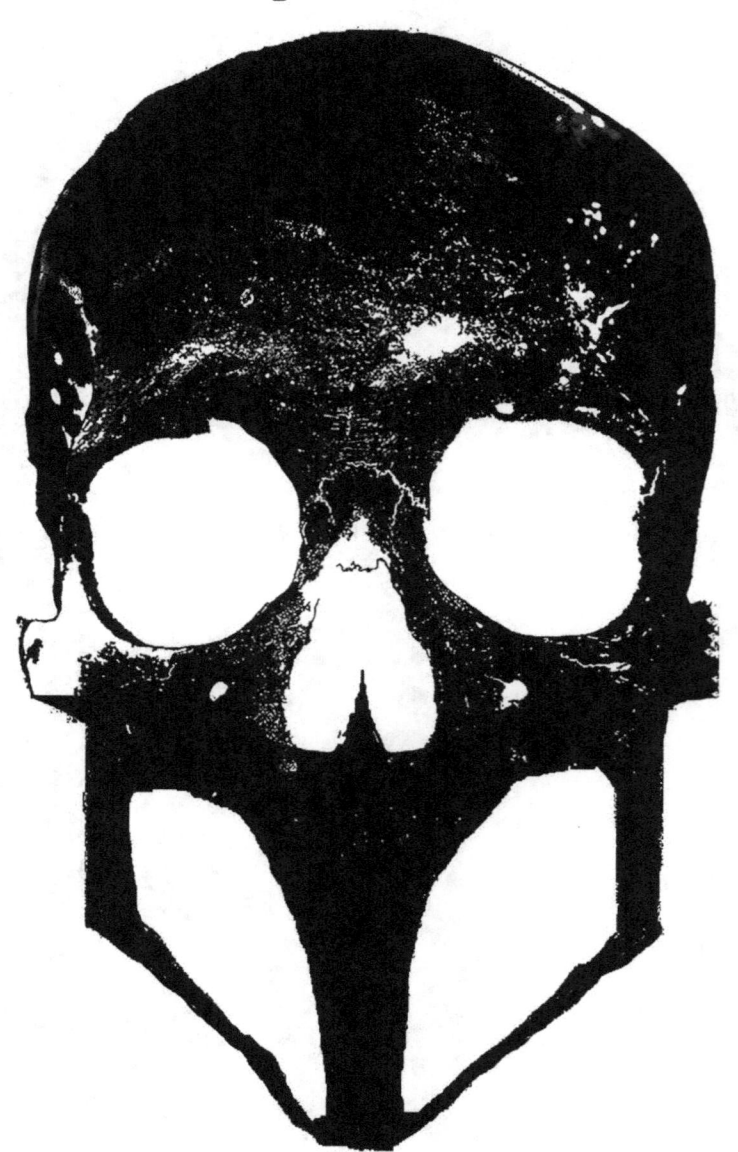

Join The Revolution

Before reading this book, first see and get to know all the incredible characters from the black devil 3 universe with the original pencil artwork drawn by the author of this book mr ossama quiader

Main characters in this book Drawn below :

Jonathon Clyde: as the Black Devil

John Michaels: as the Black Skull

Adrian Brown: as the Blue Eagle

Quick Shot: the commander of the modern league of desolation

THE BLACK DEVIL

by: Ossama Quiader

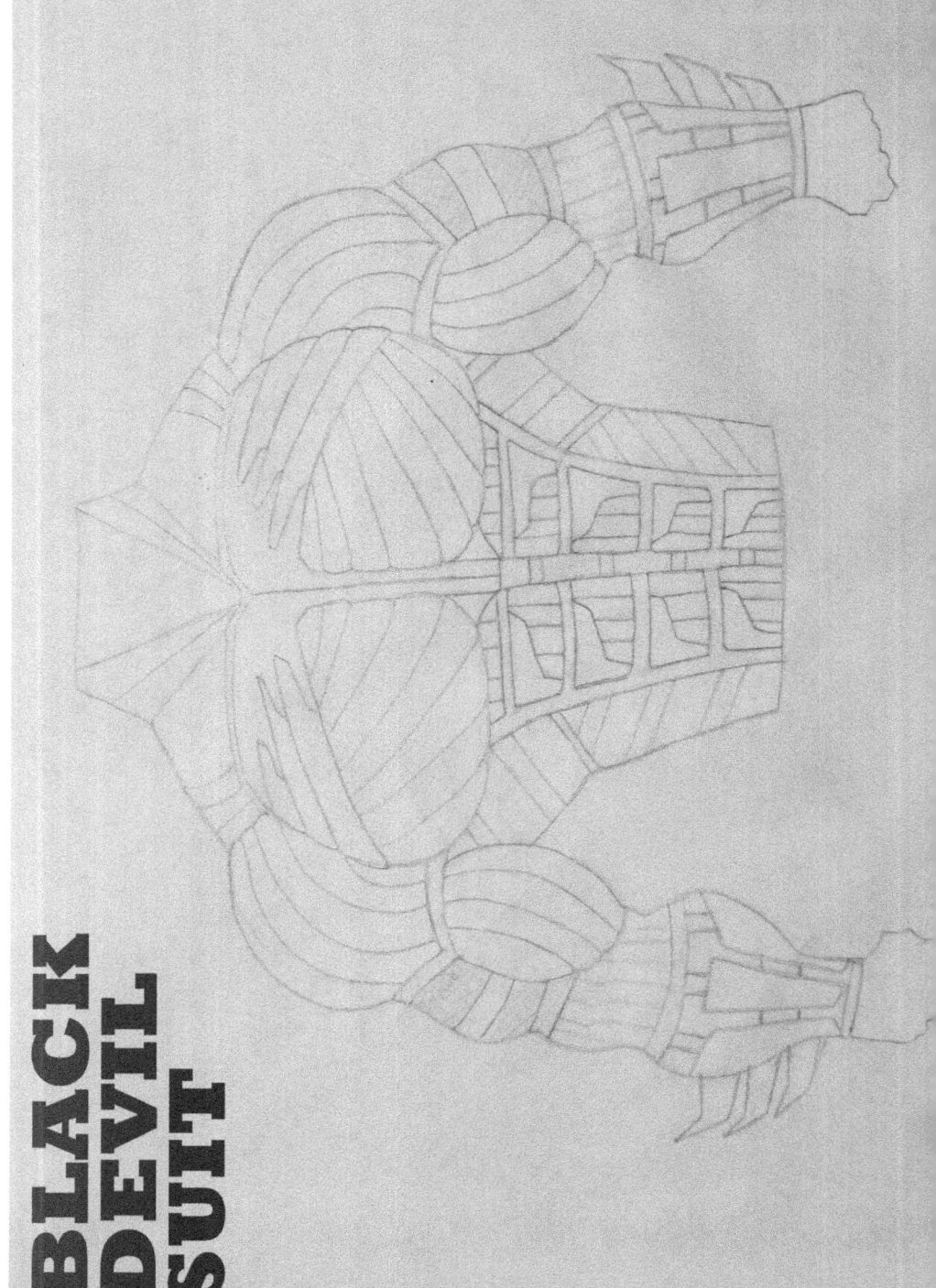

BLACK
DEVIL
SUIT

TRANSFORMED
BLACK
DEVIL

QUICK SHOT

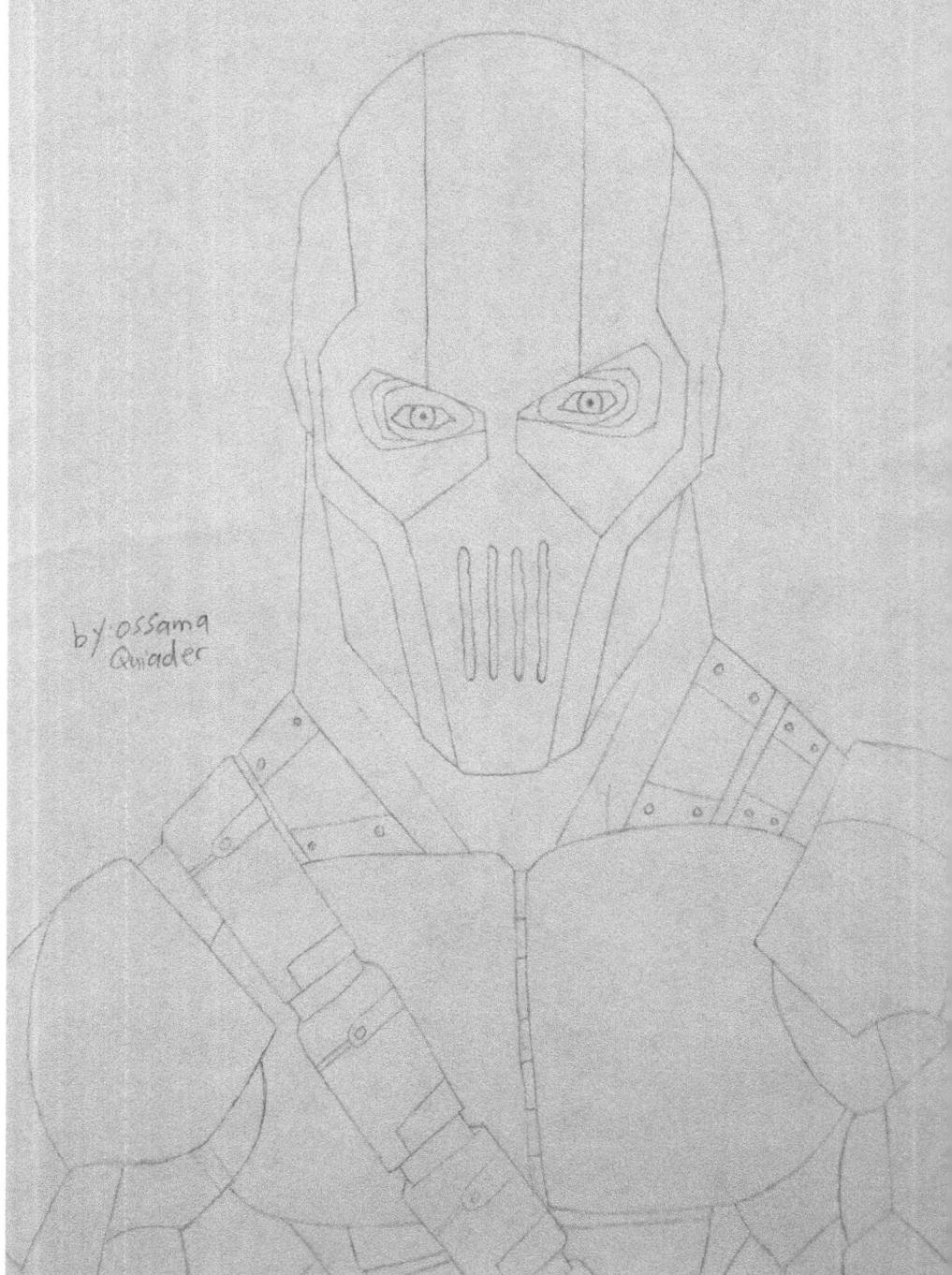

by:ossama Quiader

BLACK SKULL

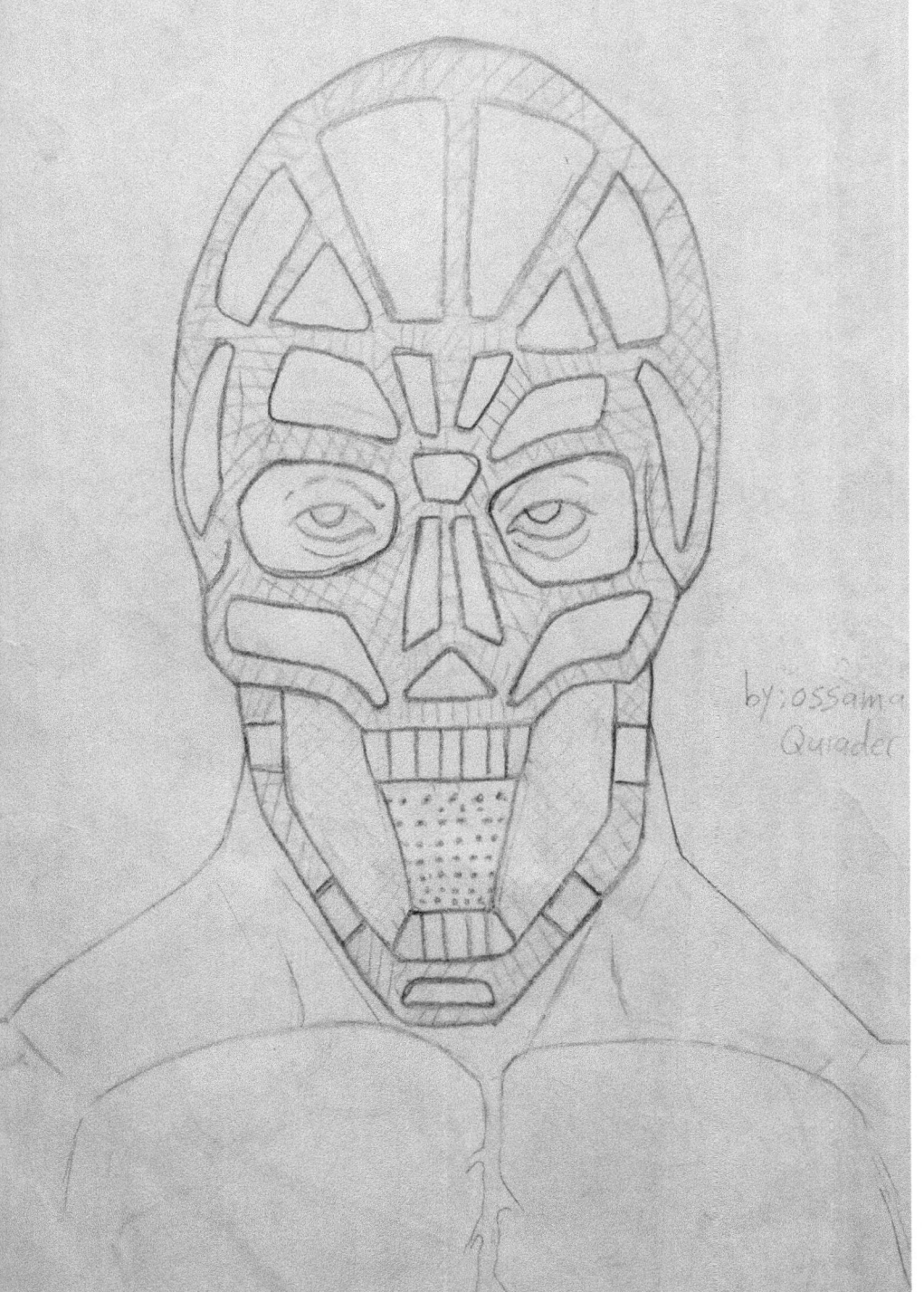

by: ossama
Quiader

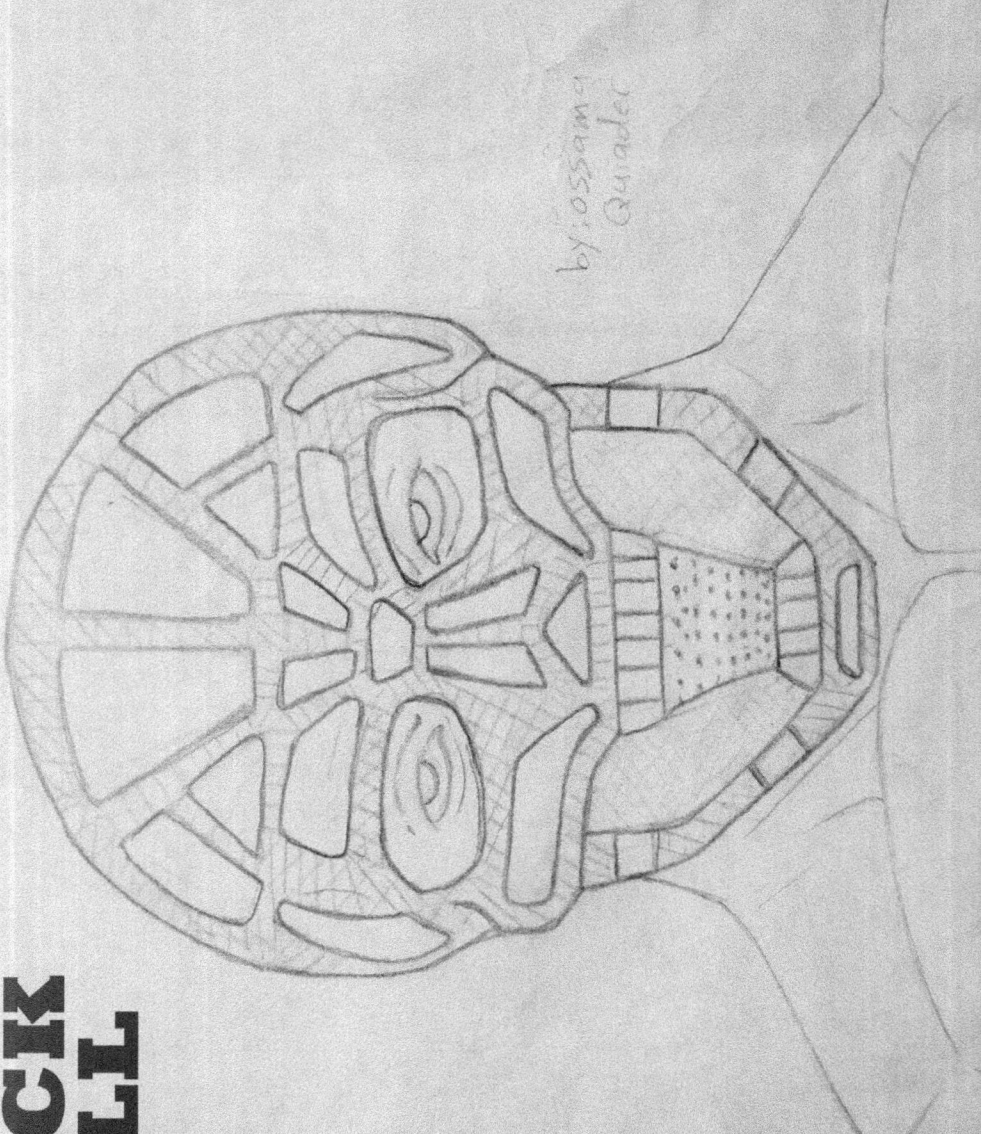

BLACK SKULL

by:ossama Quader

THE BLACK SKULL

THE BLUE EAGLE

THE BLUE EAGLE MASK

by:assamd
Quiader

THE BLUE EAGLE SUIT

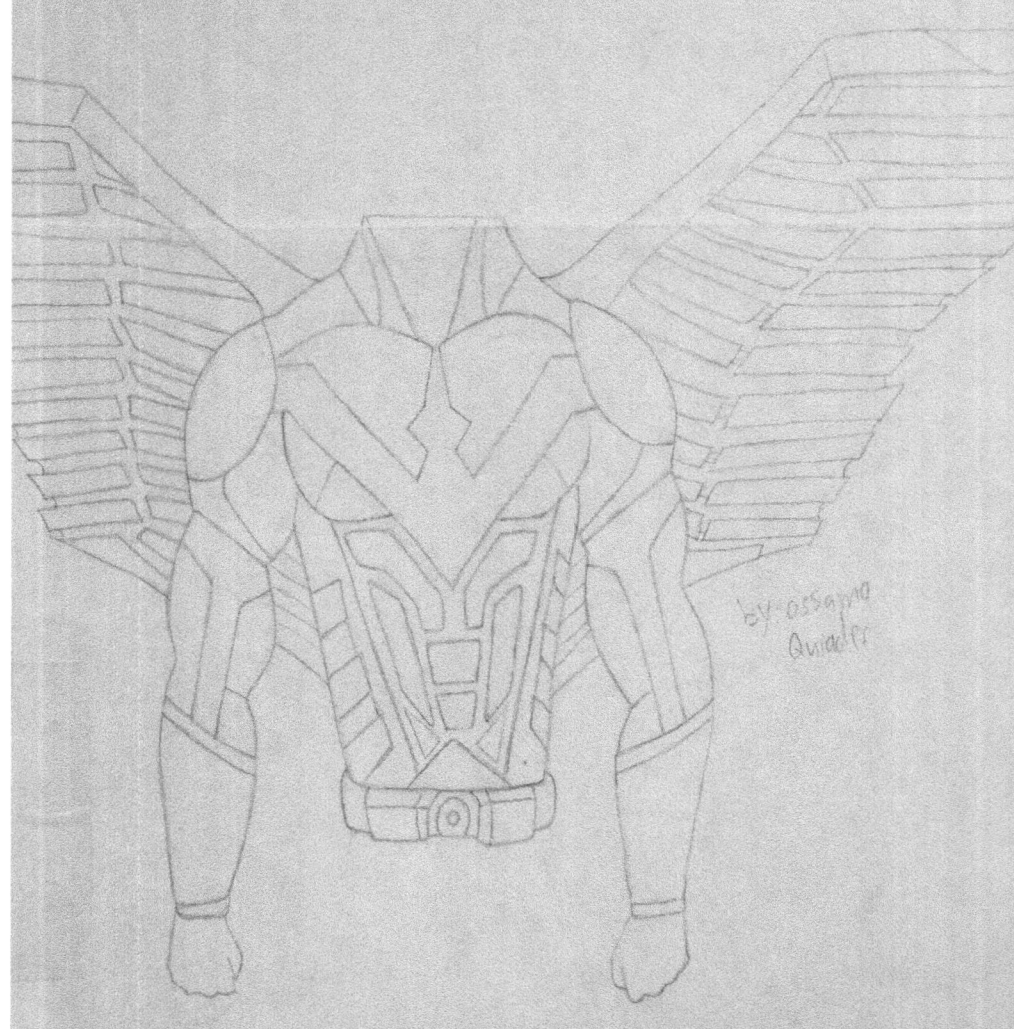

by ossama
Quader

Main characters in this book:

Jonathon Clyde: as the Black Devil

Malisa Clyde: as the Black Devil's wife

James Clyde: as the Black Devil's son

Jake Kensway: as the Mayor of Central City

Dan Michaels: as the Black Skull's father

John Michaels: as the Black Skull

Adrian Brown: as the Blue Eagle

Carlo Mankeno: as the gang boss

Quick Shot

THE BLACK DEVIL 3 AND THE REVENGE OF DESOLATION

Chapter 1: A Hero Or A Criminal

It's been five years since the horrific Central City raids and the Faker's reign of terror had come to an end, so now we find Central City is once again living in peace and after a long day of work and school families across the entire country sit down to watch some TV after dinner. Suddenly a breaking news report comes on across the country and the reporters start reporting about a strange blue man, saying:

"Sorry about interrupting your TV programs but we have a very important announcement; we have some breaking news. Last night one of the city's most feared and infamous gangs, the West Coast Killers, were partially dismantled and erased from history. Police believe about 95% of the members of the West Coast Killers gang have been murdered. More than five thousand gang members were found dead inside their hideouts, while another four thousand were found lying dead on the streets of Central City.

"Police say the one responsible for the gang's demise, and the nine thousand member death, was a strange blue man dressed like an eagle. Police are certain that this eagle vigilante is none other than Adrian Brown, an ex-prisoner who had claws and wings inside prison. Adrian Brown escaped from Central City prison three months ago and is now a fugitive on the run. Police are on the hunt but can't seem to catch him. Please be on the lookout for this man and if you see him please call Crime Stoppers at 1-800-379-851."

A week later there is a second news report about the Blue Eagle:

"The police have yet again spotted the Blue Eagle flying across the rooftops of Central City. For the past couple of weeks the Blue Eagle has been busy cleaning up crime and bringing down drug dealers and criminals. CCTV and news cameras have captured some footage, and we're about to show you some of it. Viewer discretion is advised, as some scenes may be violent and disturbing for some viewers."

Then the news shows a few short clips and warns the viewers that this man is a fugitive and might be dangerous so take caution and stay away from him, and don't forget to call Crime Stoppers if he is spotted.

For the next couple of weeks the Blue Eagle continues his criminal cleanup of Central City, and we see scene after scene of the Blue Eagle flying across the sky and snatching wanted criminals and robbers away with his sharp claws and escorting them through the sky, then placing them next to police stations where they would eventually be detained and arrested.

In other scenes the Blue Eagle would hunt down and capture rapists and serial killers, then tie them up and place them next to police stations and governmental buildings. The police would arrive and find the rapists and serial killers bleeding, bruised and badly injured, each with a note attached them indicating their crime and stating that all crime in this city will be cleaned up, so show this to all the criminals and let this be an example for all of them.

The Blue Eagle was also shown hunting down and capturing drug dealers on the streets and then taking them into a remote area, where he would torture them into telling him where their bosses and drug trafficking organizations were located. The drug dealers would break and tell him everything.

After he got the information he would fly over each location and infiltrate all the drug lords' hideouts across the entire city and then he would fight, tranquilize and tie all the bosses and their men before pouring cocaine over them, then calling the police and telling them,

"Come to these locations and arrest the drug lords, along with their drug trafficking thugs. Don't worry; they're all badly injured and tied up, so they won't give you any problems. Just come to these locations and shut down their operations. We do not need any drugs and drug dealers in this city anymore."

The police would arrive on the scene across the city and every compound they entered they find badly injured men in houses and apartments and compounds, tied up with drugs poured over them. The police would also find hundreds of kilos of drugs, stacked on tables and on floors, and writing on the walls saying, "You call me a fugitive and a vigilante but I just did what you couldn't do. All these men are drug traffickers; they are destroying lives. All the crime in this city will be cleaned up, so show this to all the drug dealers and criminals and let this be an example for all of them. Crime will not be tolerated in Central City."

The legend of the Blue Eagle gains popularity and people start talking about him. People start calling him a hero and a freedom fighter. The word spreads and then more and more newsrooms and TV talk shows start reporting and debating about the Blue Eagle, saying,

"Everyone has been talking about Adrian Brown, aka the Blue Eagle, saying he's some sort of hero. Adrian Brown is no hero; he is a murderous lunatic. He wears an eagle suit with a mask; he has sharp claws and he has wings; he flies across the roof tops of Central City hunting down, killing and torturing criminals. He thinks he can take the law into his own hands. In this country what he's doing is 100% illegal; he's a straight-out vigilante. And I would like to see him face trial and be executed in front of the whole city. This man needs to be killed ASAP."

The government speaks out:

"Central City has a new menace called the Blue Eagle. His ruthless behavior of torturing and killing criminals will not be tolerated. He is a fugitive on the run and he is a major danger to this city and America. We are putting the Blue Eagle on the most wanted list and we assure you all that we will capture this man."

Another news debate show:

"The man uses a gun. He kills people and he tortures criminals. In this country everyone deserves a fair trial and this kind of behavior cannot be tolerated.

"Well Sam, I'm afraid you're mistaken. The Blue Eagle only used real guns to kill the 9 thousand members of the West Coast Killers gang. He now uses a tranquilizing sniper; it's the same thing they use to put down rhinos and elephants in Africa, but his snipers are more powerful and more advanced. I have never seen this type of technology before. This man must be a genius, and I don't like it either, but his tactics of torturing criminals seem to be working. Sam, crime in this city has dropped by 45% and criminals are scared to death of this guy.

"James, the man is a lunatic. Like you said, he killed 9 thousand gang members and he tortures criminals and hands them over to the police. Torture and killing as you please in this country is not allowed; even the civilians are feeling fearful these days. The Blue Eagle should just leave the crime fighting to the police force. We don't need a superhuman vigilante freak like the Blue Eagle in our city. The Black Devil has been and will always be good enough to save us when trouble occurs. This new guy is just insane and the police will catch him soon."

News reports:

"The Blue Eagle strikes again, this time capturing 2 wanted criminals that have been on the run for more than 6 years, the police say. They found the fugitives in bad condition, and the Blue Eagle has taken things too far by torturing his criminals. Police say they are trying their best to find and detain the Blue Eagle, but and I quote, he is simply too elusive and too fast."

Meanwhile Jonathon Clyde has been watching the news reports at the ranch and knows all about the Blue Eagle's recent activities. While he is watching the news one day his wife comes up to him and asks him, "Jonathon, who is this Blue Eagle individual? All the news reports have been showing images of him torturing simple robbers and drug dealers. He is taking things too far. I think you need to track him down and speak to him."

Jonathon Clyde replies, "I think you're right, Malisa, he is taking things too far. I agree with everything he is doing, but torturing and killing simple criminals cannot be tolerated. I'll see what I can do."

A day later the president contacts the mayor of Central City and gives a message. The mayor then calls Jonathon Clyde and tells him to meet him in his office in the PDA apartment. Jonathon Clyde puts his suit on and heads to the mayors office, were he finds his old friend Jake Kensway, aka the mayor of Central City. Jake tells the Black Devil,

"The president gave me a call today. He told me to personally tell you that he wants you to track the Blue Eagle down and convince him to stop torturing and killing criminals and bringing fear to civilians, and if he doesn't agree to these conditions then you need to bring him in so he can be arrested and executed."

The Black Devil then says, "I agree with both the president and you, Jake: Adrian Brown is a psychopath. He must be stopped before he seriously harms anyone else. I'll find him and see what I can do."

Meanwhile the Blue Eagle is standing at the very top of a high rooftop at night, scanning for crime with his night vision ultra detection goggles. After scanning for a while he spots an old woman coming back from work. She enters an alleyway to get home and 3 guys follow her into the alleyway, looking to assault and rob her. The Blue Eagle quickly flies towards them and stands at the top of a balcony located directly in front of the alleyway, then he grabs his night vision sniper and aims it towards the thugs. The thugs begin grabbing the old lady and the Blue Eagle quickly aims his sniper and shoots the 3 thugs in the neck with tranquilizers, the thugs quickly drop to the floor and the old lady escapes.

Then the Blue Eagle hears a voice from behind saying, "Nice shot."

The Blue Eagle turns around and sees the Black Devil standing behind him. The Blue Eagle then says, "Oh, look who it is—it's the one and only the infamous Black Devil. You, sir, are a true hero and I respect you for all you have done for this city and the world. You are the one who has inspired me and many others to stand up against injustice and fight crime. So have you come to join me?"

The Black Devil then says, "Actually, I have come to deliver a message from the president himself, and the message is simple: stop torturing and killing criminals or I will have to personally bring you down and take you in to the government for execution."

"Is that so? I would like to see you try, but CAN'T YOU SEE what's happening here? The government and the police force are just jealous and afraid that they will never be able to do what I just did. The crime rate has decreased by 45% since I cleaned up this city and many other criminals have stopped their evil ways because they know what I will do to them, if I find them. The criminals are living in fear and that's exactly what I want. You see, you cannot be merciful to these people. The government and the police force have been slapping these criminals gently on the wrist and treating them nicely for years and where did that get them? Nowhere. When the criminals do not fear the consequences of their crimes, they will continue killing robbing, vandalizing and selling drugs because they know when they get caught nothing is going to happen to them. Once they get caught, these criminals need to all be taught a lesson and given a taste of their own medicine."

"I completely disagree; all you need to do is capture and hand the criminals over to the authorities, and they will punish them accordingly. There is no need to murder and torture these people. I don't understand why you're extremely violent and ruthless towards criminals."

"You want to know why I'm so violent towards criminals? You want to know why I hate them so much? I'll tell you why. My name is Adrian Brown and I was born as a superhuman. I came into the world with sharp claws and wings attached to my back. The doctors said I was a half human-half eagle mutant but my parents did not care; they still loved me and raised me. My family was very poor and we lived in a poor and bad neighborhood, full of violence, gangs and drugs. When I was around 12 years old my father suffered a back injury and couldn't work anymore so as time went on our money ran out and we become bankrupt and in serious financial debt. The bank and the government came and took everything from us; they took our house, our furniture and everything else. We had nothing left.

"So now we had 2 choices: either suffer and die on the streets, or do whatever it took to survive.

"We chose plan B. My parents did the unthinkable: they made us join a powerful gang called the West Coast Killers. The gang boss, who was named Carlo Mankeno, took us in and because of my parents' innocence and my superhuman capabilities the gang decided to take advantage of us. They forced me and my family to murder people, rob shops and sell drugs, and we couldn't say no because the gang would have killed us or even worse, badly tortured us if we refused their orders, and their number one rule was once you join the gang there is no getting out, so it was kill or be killed. We had no choice; my family and I killed many people and destroyed many lives with the heroine and drugs we were selling, but because of the gang life we made a lot of money and rented a small house.

"But shortly after the gang started secretly drugging us and we soon became addicted, and the gang life after that became our life. We all became evil and our souls were lost. One day my father and mother were making a large drug delivery late at night, and they got robbed. They came back to the compound and the boss, Carlo Mankeno, was furious, because he just lost millions of dollars on that deal, and now his associates overseas are all angry and demanding a complete refund of their money. so the next day Carlo Mankeno drugged me and started telling me lies about my parents, which made me extremely angry, then he told me, "'Grab a gun and go kill your parents, and if you disobey my orders I will torture you and then I will kill you."

"At that time my brain was gone and I was insane from all the violence I had seen and all the drugs I had taken. I really wasn't thinking straight at all and I was afraid, so to prove my loyalty to the gang I quickly grabbed a gun, entered my parents' home and shot them both dead. I saw both my parents' bodies drop to the ground and their blood spill out in front of me. The boss and the other gang members came into the house and started laughing; that's when the reality hit me. I started crying and I couldn't believe what I had just done. The drugs and the violence had turned me into someone I'm not, but it was too late now. The police shortly arrived and I was sentenced to 70 years in prison. I entered prison regretting everything I had done, and from that day on I decided to completely change and become better, and I promised myself that I wasn't going to allow what happened to me happen to anyone else. I promised that once I escaped prison I was going to kill all the West Coast Killer gang and then I was going to rid Central City and eventually the world of all its crime and criminals.

"I spent 8 years in prison, then around 5 years ago the Faker came along and the Central City raids happened. Throughout the entire Faker events I used to watch the news podcasts and news reports and sometimes I would see you, in your Black Devil costume, fighting crime and defending the people, putting your life on the line every time just to protect others. You were a furious beast and a true warrior, and every time I saw you, you inspired me. You were using your superhuman ability to help others and protect the weak, and that's when I truly found my purpose in life. The entire time I was using my powers do terrible things and harm others, when I could have been using my powers to help people. I truly regretted all the things I did and I wanted to make things right for all my past mistakes but in order to clean up Central City I first had to escape from prison, and about 4 months after the Faker's death my chance came.

"Inside prison my wings where always restrained with a metal brace attachment, but one Tuesday morning I woke up with parasites in my stomach and the pain I felt was just unimaginable. The prison guards came into my cell and quickly took me to the prison hospital, and inside the hospital they gave me sleeping gas and took the metal brace off my wings, then they handcuffed my hands to the bed and began treating me. The next day, I woke up felling healthy again and nobody was in the room. I was all alone, and the metal brace attachment was removed and my wings were free, and the only thing that was holding me was 2 metal handcuffs. The prison guards must have thought that I wasn't capable of breaking handcuffs but they were wrong. I knew this was my only chance to escape, so I broke the handcuffs, spread my wings and walked out of the room. Then I headed towards the exit door. Some guards tried to stop me but they were no match for me. I knocked them all unconscious then I went outside the prison hospital, spread my wings and flew away to freedom.

"Then I hid out at a friend's house for a couple of days. My friend owned a high tech weapons and armory shop. He made high-tech guns, Kevlar armor and protective clothing. He gave me all the material and we made a high grade costume with a mask to protect my identity. He made me some guns and then I was ready. I then proceeded to locate and kill the entire West Coast Killers gang. I firstly tracked down tortured and killed Carlo Mankeno, the gang boss who caused me and my family unimaginable pain and misery. I killed him and all his top ranked men, then one by one I tracked down and killed nearly all the West Coast Killers gang members inside their hideouts and on the streets of Central City. The police didn't know who the killer was until just 2 months ago because I was simply too elusive; I covered my tracks well. And since then I've been capturing, torturing and killing criminals, and I will continue my crusade until this city and eventually the world is free from all crime, drugs and criminals. I will make sure that no one goes through what my family and I went through.

"So I'm sorry to disappoint you but I won't stop what I'm doing until the crime rate in this city drops by 100%. Now get out of my way, or I will have to use force."

The Black Devil then says, "I now understand your hatred towards criminals but I'm afraid I can't let you torture and kill as you please in this city. You leave me no choice: either surrender peacefully or I will take you in by force."

The Blue Eagle then says, "I won't allow anyone to stand in the way of accomplishing my mission, not even you." The Blue Eagle then flies up, aims his sniper and shoots the Black Devil. The Black Devil rolls to the side and avoids the bullets, he grabs his grappling hook and fires it towards the Blue Eagle. The rope from the grappling hook attaches to the Blue Eagle's arm & begins to shock him. The Blue Eagle falls down, & the Black Devil uses the attached rope to swing and slam the Blue Eagle against the concrete balcony and metal railing of the rooftop. The Blue Eagle then grabs the attached rope and pulls the Black Devil towards him, the Blue Eagle then grabs and throws the Black Devil into the concrete door of the rooftop. The entire structure breaks, the Blue Eagle flies towards him, grabs him again and slams him into the concrete floor. The Black Devil quickly gets up & throws a sonic electricity bomb at the Blue Eagle. The bomb explodes and slightly injures the Blue Eagle. The Black Devil then throws 5 smoke bombs on the ground and the entire rooftop fills with dark smoke. The Black Devil stops for a moment & says in a loud, angry voice, "We don't need to do this. Just give yourself up and I'll take you in peacefully. I don't want to hurt you."

The Blue Eagle Replies in an equally loud, angry voice, "You will never take me in even if you try, and you think your smoke will hide you from me? Have you forgotten that I'm an eagle hybrid with superior eagle vision?"

The Blue Eagle then blinks; everything around him turns blue and he starts seeing the Black Devil moving side to side through the smoke, coming towards him. The Black Devil then jumps up and throws a spinning kick. The Blue

Eagle flies back and dodges the kick, then quickly flies back into the smoke, rushes towards the Black Devil and starts hitting him with some quick and devastating spinning and flying attacks. The Black Devil tries to defend himself but fails to do so; he drops to the ground, then quickly gets up and starts punching and kicking the Blue Eagle. The Blue Eagle tries to fend off the attacks and fights back; he expands his claws and starts viciously slashing out at the Black Devil. The Black Devil dodges most of the claw attacks but eventually gets slashed across the face and across the chest on the 2 final hits.

Both men trade punches and kicks inside the dark smoke until the Blue Eagle suddenly trips the Black Devil with a wing attack and slams him hard into the concrete floor. The Black Devil drops to the ground, dazed, & hurt he slowly gets up and finds the Blue Eagle floating high above him. The Blue Eagle then grabs his sniper rifle and starts shooting at the Black Devil. The Black Devil sees the bullets coming and starts moving and rolling from side to side and hiding behind objects in order to avoid getting shot. The Black Devil then throws more smoke bombs onto the rooftop in order to make it difficult for the Blue Eagle to shoot him. Then, from within the smoke, the Black Devil grabs his devil triton and starts firing back at the Blue Eagle. The Blue Eagle DOESN'T see some of the blasts coming and gets hit with an energy ray, which injures him and launches him backwards into the air. The Blue Eagle becomes angry and says in a loud voice, "This ends now."

The Blue Eagle spreads his wings and flies towards the Black Devil, The Black Devil starts firing energy rays from his triton but the Blue Eagle dodges the blasts and flies into the smoke, grabs the Black Devil by his neck, and flies him upwards into the sky and while in mid air, the Blue Eagle lets go and allows the Black Devil to drop. While in free fall the Blue Eagle rushes up and begins to punch the Black Devil, then grabs him from his waist and uses the Black Devil's back to break through the rooftop ceiling, the Blue Eagle keeps flying downwards and breaks nine floors of the building's ceilings with the Black Devil's back and spine. The Black Devil feels the effects and starts screaming in pain, then his veins begin to boil, the color of his skin turns red and the Black Devil begins transforming into a huge red devil monster with horns and wings. The transformed Devil then grabs and throws the Blue Eagle through the window of a nearby office building. The Blue Eagle breaks and goes through the glass, the concrete columns and some office tables and appliances. The transformed Devil then flies towards the Blue Eagle, grabs him and throws him across the room into more office appliances, and concrete columns.

The transformed Devil then looks at the Blue Eagle and releases a beam of fire from his mouth. The Blue Eagle quickly moves away and the fire beam hits and breaks most of the floor's supporting reinforcement structure. The top of the building becomes unstable and begins to collapse and burn. The Blue Eagle panics and tries to find a way out. The transformed Devil begins to follow and chase him from behind trying to grab him, the Blue Eagle starts moving away and try's to escape but every time the Blue Eagle finds an opening to escape a large piece of concrete metal and fire drops from above and blocks his way, but the Blue Eagle desperately keeps on trying and eventually finds an opening and flies out of the building, the Black Devil also tries to escape but doesn't quite make it in time and half of the building collapses on top of him and injuries him badly. The Blue Eagle takes a deep breath and thinks it's all over.

But then the transformed Black Devil breaks through all the concrete, metal and fire and flies towards the Blue Eagle and starts chasing him. The Blue Eagle becomes terrified and starts flying away and heads to the main streets of Central City, then the Blue Eagle stats zigzagging and flying in between buildings in order to escape from the transformed Devil but the transformed Devil stays within range and starts launching fire from his hands and mouth towards the Blue Eagle. The Blue Eagle quickly evades the fire attacks, but the Black Devil quickly rushes towards him and grabs his arm. The Blue Eagle reacts quickly; he does a back flip and kicks the transformed Black Devil hard to the chin. The Black Devil feels the impact and starts lashing out at the Blue Eagle. The Blue Eagle becomes terrified and starts dodging the attacks. The transformed Black Devil then grabs the Blue Eagle's leg and launches him hard into a nearby building. The Blue Eagle hits the building hard and the transformed Black Devil quickly flies towards him. The Black Devil comes extremely close and gets ready to punch the Blue Eagle but just before the punch could land the Blue Eagle quickly flies upwards and the transformed Black Devil goes right through the building,

The transformed Black Devil comes out of the building and once again starts chasing the Blue Eagle. The Blue Eagle becomes terrified and starts flying away.

The Blue Eagle starts flying in between buildings at full speed. The transformed Devil follows him from behind, then all of a sudden the Blue Eagle flies straight at maximum speed. The Black Devil also increases his speed and tries to catch up to the Blue Eagle but then suddenly and unexpectedly, the Blue Eagle makes a very sharp left turn. He turns his body to the side and flies through a narrow gap in between 2 buildings and escapes the scene. The transformed Devil stumbles and also makes the fast turn, not realizing that the gap is far too small for him to fit through, so he ends up brutally crashing in between the 2 narrow buildings. His body breaks the concrete and the reinforcement steel and he falls hard into the ground, moments later the 2 halves of the building come crashing on top of him. The injuries from breaking through the 2 buildings and the collapsing concrete injure the transformed Black Devil badly but he manages to remove the concrete debris off himself and gets free. He escapes the scene & passes out on top of a building and starts transforming back into his normal form. Ten minutes later he wakes up and travels home to the cattle ranch, where he starts recovering and healing his wounds.

For the next couple of weeks the Blue Eagle is not seen by anybody and he is pronounced possibly dead or on the run by the media and the government.

(Now we must go back 10 years into the past to fully understand the story.)

10 years earlier...

Chapter 2: A loud cry in Central City 10 years ago

Ten years earlier, in Central City on a normal Monday morning, we find a man named Dan Michaels and his 13-year-old son John Michaels begging for food in the main streets of Central City. After begging and trying to survive on the streets for hours, Dan and his son only make 9 dollars. The father gets up off the floor and tells his boy,

"Come on, son, 9 dollars is good enough. We'll grab a bite to eat then we'll go home."

But as they are walking towards the shops a drug dealer comes out of the alleyway and robs them. He takes their money and both their jackets and then he runs away. Panicked, hungry and afraid, Dan Michaels and his son John quickly rush home. Now Dan and his son don't live in an ordinary home; they live in an abandoned, broken-down house, which was heavily damaged by a house fire and hurricanes. Both the son and the father enter their home. After a while night falls and they sleep.

While in deep sleep Dan Michaels and his 13-year-old son John suddenly hear a loud gunshot inside their home and they quickly get up, then they hear a loud voice coming from the darkness: "Wake up, Dan Michaels, your time has come; your time ends here." The father and the son suddenly wake up, shocked and fearful. Dan Michaels replies, "Who's there? Please, who are you? We don't want any trouble. I have my son here; just please leave us alone." The dark voice replies, "Did you leave us alone when we begged for mercy? NO. I told you I was coming for you all; I told you I was going to hunt you all down one by one." Dan Michaels then says, "Oh, it's you. I know exactly who you are." The Black Devil then says, "So you remember me now." Dan Michaels says, "Yes, but how can this be? I thought they killed you a long time ago." The Black Devil then says, "NO, I'm still alive and you're the last of them; after you die the League will be history, gone forever. The League will finally be a long distant memory and this world will be a safer place for everyone."

Then the Black Devil throws a disk on the ground. The black disk opens up and starts to spin, then the spinning disk begins to release blinding, powerful flashes of blue and white light. The entire house starts flashing with blinding rays. Dan Michaels' 13-year-old son begins to cry and scream loudly, saying, "DAD, HELP ME, I'M SCARED." Dan Michaels then grabs his gun from under the mattress and tells his son in a loud voice, "LET'S GET OUT OF HERE. COME ON, LET'S GO–RUN." The Black Devil then drops from the ceiling and starts chasing Dan Michaels. When Dan Michaels sees him coming from behind, he becomes extremely terrified and starts running and shooting bullets and spikes from his hands, then all of a sudden the sky begins to rain heavily, and as the bullets and spikes pass, the Black Devil quickly moves and shoots a grappling rope towards the building next to him. The rope automatically pulls him up to the rooftop of the building, where the Black Devil presses a button on his belt and his shoes turn blue underneath.

The blue modern technology shoes allow the Black Devil to automatically stick to any surface, and it also allows him to run and move much faster. The Black Devil then quickly starts chasing Dan Michaels from the rooftops and manages to catch up with him easily.

Meanwhile, Dan Michaels is running on the streets of Central City below. He looks back and he sees the Black Devil chasing him from the rooftops; then, out of fear, Dan makes a stupid decision and runs into a dead-end alleyway. The Black Devil then jumps down from the building and comes face to face with Dan. Then Dan aims his hand towards the Black Devil and tells him in a frightened voice, "Stay back, stay back." Then Dan starts shooting spikes from his hands. The spikes race towards the Black Devil, but the Black Devil quickly deploys a blue energy shield from his hand, which stops the spikes from hitting him. Suddenly John Michaels comes running into the alleyway, crying and screaming, "Please don't kill my dad; he's the only family I have. Don't kill him, please."

The Black Devil looks back to see the crying boy. Dan Michaels quickly takes advantage of the situation and aims his gun, but just before Dan can fire the Black Devil uses his magnetic impulse glove to snatch the gun out of Dan's hand from a distance of 30 meters. The Black Devil then uses the gun and shoots Dan Michaels 7 times in the chest. While witnessing his father getting shot John Michaels screams, "NOOOOO DAD." Dan Michaels' body drops to the ground; the son runs towards his dad's body and The Black Devil escapes the scene by running up the wall. John Michaels then grabs his dad's head and tells him, "Please Dad, don't leave me; you're all I've got. Stay with me, Dad, please." Dan Michaels looks at his son and with his dying words he says, "No son, my time has come. You must stay strong now. Don't forget me; always keep me in your memories, and if you can, avenge my death, and kill the Black Devil and most importantly, don't let the League of Desolation die. Continue our legacy, and fulfill our destiny." Then his eyes close and he dies. John Michael starts to cry deeply, while the rain is pouring down on him. Ten minutes later the police arrive. They take John Michaels away and cover his dad's dead body with a white cloth.

Chapter 3: The hardships of life

After the incident John Michaels gets taken to the police station, where they allow him spend a few nights in their open prison cells while they sort out some place for him to stay. After 2 days of searching the police decide to put John Michaels with his new foster parents. They place him with his aunt Marley Michaels and her husband Ram Isaac. He is placed with his aunt and her husband because John Michael's mother was murdered when he was just a young boy.

Now Marley Michaels absolutely hated her brother Dan Michaels because he was responsible for the death of one of their brothers. She always called him a good for nothing bum, a crook and a filthy criminal. So John Michaels' foster parents and their children treated him very badly, hitting and screaming at him constantly, and because of the foster parents' treatment, John Michaels decides to leave and run away from the family home. So one night he packs his bags quietly, jumps out the window and runs away, then he takes some time and looks around Central City. After hours of searching he finds a bridge to live under. During the day he would spend his time begging on the streets and at night he would sleep in the cold under Central City's bridge with 20 other homeless people. Life on streets is absolutely miserable for a 13-year-old kid, and his difficult life on the street eventually leads him to a life of crime and drug trafficking. In the beginning he starts working for a small gang selling small amounts of drugs and weapons, but eventually, after drug trafficking for many years, he manages to become the king of the drug underworld. He gets a name for himself and becomes known as Central City's most wanted, most recognized and most feared criminal. Five years later, on a Monday afternoon, he orders his men to buy him a durable bulletproof skeleton mask from the local mask maker. His men do as they were ordered and bring him the mask. After he receives his mask, the Black Skull goes inside his office and pours hot industrial glue on his face and puts on the black skeleton mask to show his darkness and hatred for society.

Then 8 months later, new drug trafficking competition tries to overrun Black Skull's industry. He takes action and kills them all. Undercover cops get the evidence they need and finally arrest him.

Black Skull attends court to hear his sentencing. A judge named Alex tells him for first class murder and countless drug trafficking offenses, "You, John Michaels, are sentenced to a lifetime of imprisonment with no chance of parole." After hearing this the Black Skull becomes outraged. He starts screaming and looks for a way to escape. The security guards grab him and escort him out of the courthouse, but before Black Skull leaves the courthouse door, he turns to Alex, the judge, and tells him in a loud voice, "YOU'RE A DEAD MAN, believe me, you're a dead man walking; we will find you and we will kill you."

Present day after the disappearance of the Blue Eagle: It was at this time, when the Black Skull entered prison, that the Blue Eagle was fighting the Black Devil and disappeared from Central City.

Chapter 4: Central City prison

A few hours later Black Skull enters Central City prison with his mask on because it is stuck to his skin and if it comes off he'll die. Inside prison, he meets 5 tough-looking men who were captured by the police force during the Central City raids. The Black Skull confronts them. He introduces himself and tells them his name and they quickly recognize him from his father, Dan Michaels. Then the leader of the group gets up and tells the Black Skull, "Your father was one of the great commanders of the League of Desolation. He was a great man. How is your father doing now? Where is he?" The Black Skull replies with a sad voice, "My father is dead." The leader gets shocked by the news and says, "What? How can this be? Who killed him?" The Black Skull replies, "It was the Black Devil." The leader of the group, whose name is Quick Shot, gets an angry look on his face and says, "The Black Devil has been our number one enemy for years now. He has killed many of our men, and he has foiled our plans many times. He thinks the League of Desolation is dead but he is greatly mistaken; within the prisons we are growing every day. We will soon make our escape and we will be unstoppable. Did your father ever tell you about us?"

The Black Skull replies, "Yes, he spoke many good things about the League and he did leave me with a final message; he said, 'Avenge my death, kill the Black Devil and don't let the League of Desolation die. Continue our legacy and fulfill our destiny."

The leader of the group, Quick Shot, becomes happy and says, "Then join us, brother, join the League of Desolation and we will make your vision and your father's vision into a reality. With your help, your money and your power we will finally fulfill our destiny and become the true and unmatched leaders of the world." The Black Skull agrees to join them. They all shake hands and they walk off into the prison's outdoor area.

The League of Desolation leaders know that the Black Skull is the right person to kill the Black Devil and finally fulfill the League's destiny of becoming great leaders. Quick Shot, the leader of the group, decides to train him. They take him to the courtyard then they hand him a hard metal stick. Black Skull then says, "Shall we begin training?" Before he can even finish his sentence he gets hit in the face with the stick, then Black Skull tells Quick Shot, "I wasn't ready." Quick Shot gets angry, rushes up and hits him rapidly while saying, "Ready? You think the prisoners will wait for you to be ready? You must always remain vigilant and ready. We will train you and the prisoners will learn to fear you like they fear us. Weakness will not be tolerated; we will push you to your limits and beyond. We will break you and then we will rebuild you." During training, they allow Black Skull to lift extremely heavy weights in the prison gym. They also teach him how to fight one person and defend against several opponents with and without blindfolds. He also learns how to defend against knife and gun attacks.

After training, Quick Shot and Black Skull sit together to talk. Black Skull starts the conversation and says, "So, tell me a bit about yourself--why are you in prison?" Quick

Shot says, "It's a long story but I and the rest of my men came here during the Central City raid, when the Faker and rest of his Rebel army were trying to conquer Central City by killing its innocent people and bringing terror to the weak and helpless. We as the League of Desolation couldn't allow that to happen, so we intervened." Then the Black Skull asks, "Who were the Rebels?"

Quick Shot then says, "The group's full name is the League of Rebellion and they have been around for centuries, but at the time when the League of Desolation was first formed, an opposing group of brave men, mostly of European origin, came into our country and rebelled against our government, and they started attacking us. We quickly took military action and attacked them back and for almost 200 years we fought against the infamous Rebels in a bloody, all-out war. We, the League of Desolation, rejected all the evil ideologies of the League of Rebellion. The great leaders of the League of Desolation used to always say that the Rebels were a bunch of insane maniacs who kill and destroy for no reason. Their only objective is to rule the world and kill the innocent and the weak. The League of Desolation is different; we only target the criminals and the evil governments of the world.

"But this is not the case with the Rebels. The League of Rebellion has killed millions of innocent people throughout the ages. They prey upon and take advantage of the weak. Another difference between us and them is that we, the League of Desolation, want to kill and replace the evil governments of the world, but the League of Rebellion would rather use the evil governments of the world to their advantage.

"We were sworn enemies so we had to stop them. During the Central City raids I and my men came to Central City when the Faker was attacking. He was killing the innocent and destroying Central City and we couldn't allow that to happen, so we came here illegally by boats in the middle of the night and we ended up in the far east of the Central City coast while the Black Devil and the Faker were at war in the western region of Central City.

"When we got off the boats we quickly attacked and we managed to kill a few hundred League of Rebellion members but in the end my men and I were captured and arrested by the police force, and they put us into Central City prisons along with the remaining League of Rebellion members. But within the prisons we killed nearly all of them, and the ones we did not kill were transferred to another prison. And that's how my men and I ended up in prison."

The Black Skull says, "My father used to tell me about Aljabaar Lucifer and Damien Black but I want to know more about them."

Quick Shot replies, "Aljabaar Lucifer, also known as the Red Devil, and Damien Black were a father-and-son team and they were the modern leaders of the League of Desolation and the leaders of the country of Mali in the Sahara desert. My brother and I were the Red Devil's right-hand men. The Red Devil and his son Damien Black were our masters; they trained us and made us into truly skilled warriors."

Black Skull then asks, "Who is your brother?" Quick Shot replies, "His name was Razor, and our story goes way back. My brother Razor and I were born in a small village located in the Sahara desert. Our parents were very poor villagers who couldn't afford to keep us, so they handed us over to the League of Desolation. The League kindly took us in and they became our new family. They fed us, they protected us and they used to train us in the art of military combat nearly every day. The training was brutal, but I remained humble, and I was always a loyal member who supported and respected the League. My brother Razor, on the other hand, had no respect; he disobeyed our leaders many times during his training. The leaders warned him many times but he would not listen; he still showed disrespect to the League, and one day during practice things got out of hand and he brutally killed one of his team members and training partners and for this reason he was sentenced to a lifetime in prison, but 5 years later the League leaders came to him one day and told him, 'We will allow you to go free, but on one condition: you must infiltrate and bring back the secrets of the League of Rebellion.' Razor agreed, and the leaders sent my brother Razor to the headquarters of the League of Rebellion, where he was acting in disguise so he could spy on them and bring back useful information. The League of Rebellion accepted Razor and allowed him into their compound, not knowing he was actually a spy. Razor trained with the Rebels and learned many of their secrets and plans, but after a couple of months the League of Rebellion found out Razor's secret. They captured my brother, put him in prison and tortured him.

"We received the news and I begged the leaders of the League of Desolation to go and save him but they refused every time; they said he was nothing but a lost cause who deserved nothing but punishment and disgrace. I couldn't just sit back while my brother was inside prison, so I decided to save him myself. The next day I headed straight for the Rebels' headquarters and I did the unthinkable. I reasoned with the enemy and I told them, 'If you let me and my brother go free, in return I will give you what you want most--a large quantity of our leader's rebel serum.' The League of Rebellion couldn't refuse my tempting offer and they agreed, but never trust a snake. They quickly broke their promise and they threw me and my brother Razor inside a large underground prison for 7 years, but eventually our prison was finally found and we were saved by none other than your father, Dan Michaels, and the remaining League of Desolation members who escaped and had survived the attacks of both the Rebels and the Black Devil.

"Then I, your father and the rest of the remaining members returned to our compound and we found it in absolute ruin. The rebels and the Black Devil destroyed everything we had ever worked for, and they killed nearly all the League of Desolation members. My brother Razor and I then went up to the mountains and we retrieved the last few drops of the rebel serum. We injected it into our bloodstream and we both gained incredible powers, then we had our last talk, shook each other's hands and went our separate ways, and I haven't seen him since that day, although he was very dear to me. But he is dead now."

Black Skull asks, "Who killed him?" Quick Shot says, "The Black Devil killed him, the same person who killed your father Dan Michaels, but don't worry; we will soon have our revenge." Then Quick Shot gets up and leaves.

Chapter 5: It's now or never

Life in prison continues and then, five years after Black Skull's training, he gets involved in a prison fight and gets stabbed several times by 2 of the Latino inmates. Quick Shot's men come to the rescue before any more fatal attacks occur. Quick Shot then grabs the Black Skull and quickly takes him to the prison hospital. After about two weeks of surgery and rest Black Skull makes a full recovery, and he is put back in prison, then 2 weeks later Quick Shot and the leaders of the League of Desolation decide to escape, so they come up with a plan.

A day later the League of Desolation starts a massive prison riot and stab the 2 Latino inmates. When officers come into the prison to fix the situation, Black Skull, Quick Shot and the rest of their men start fighting and sneaking through the prison riot, the League of Desolation begin grabbing the prisoners and smashing them into and through the cafeteria tables, chairs and glass. After seeing this more prisoners and officers begin attacking them, the League of Desolation quickly retaliate and dismantle the oncoming attackers with heavy punches kicks and elbows. They then locate and kill 5 riot control officers, take their keys and proceed towards the exit. The prison has three main gates. They open the first gate then shut it so no one else can get out, because the other inmates are not part of the League and they are useless to them. Then the League of Desolation proceed to the second gate. They open it and the Black Skull walks toward the third gate alone, with the leaders of the League of Desolation hiding behind the second gate walls so they can't be seen. Three officers come through the third gate, screaming at Black Skull, "Put your hands behind your head and get on the ground." The Black Skull puts his hands behind his head and gets on his knees. The officers come over grab his hands and proceed to handcuff him. The League of Desolation members quickly rush towards the prison officers and break their necks. They then proceed to the third and final gate, where they get to the front of the prison. At the front they see fencing and 2 prison towers, with guards aiming snipers at them. The guards in the towers say in a loud voice,

"WE ARE GOING TO GIVE YOU EXACTLY 10 SECONDS TO GET BACK INTO THE PRISON; AFTER 10 SECONDS IF YOU ARE NOT INSIDE THE PRISON WE WILL SHOOT YOU." The guards start counting, "10, 9, 8, 7, 6 , 5, 4 , 3," but before the guards could count to 2 and get a chance to shoot, the prison tower guards get shot from behind by sniper-wielding men who are hiding inside the bushes outside the prison gate. (These men where pre-hired by the Black Skull.) The prison guards die and drop on the floor, then the pre-hired men cut a hole in the fence and the Black Skull, his crew and the rest of League of Desolation members all get into the pre-hired cars and drive away. While driving Black Skull starts reminiscing about his father; he starts remembering all the good things his father had done for him in his life, a tear drops from his eye and he becomes silently angry.

Chapter 6: Life on the outside

One week After prison break Black Skull and the League of Desolation find a hideout in an abandoned warehouse. After they arrive Quick Shot brings out a metal suitcase. He opens it and inside there is a small bottle of liquid and a syringe filled with blue moving, sparkling particles. The Black Skull says, "What is this?"

Quick Shot replies, "It's the Rebel serum. The founders of the League of Desolation found a large puddle filled with this strange substance long ago. They found it high up in the desert mountains. This needle contains the last few drops, and I've been saving for someone special and I've decided to give it to you."

Black Skull then says, "What does this substance do?"

Quick Shot replies, "Once this substance is injected into the body it gives ordinary men extraordinary powers. Your father took this substance and that is why he could release sharp wooden spikes from his hands. My brother, my masters and I have also been injected. This serum allows you to live for hundreds of years without aging. I, your father and anyone else who has taken this serum or the devil serum are much, much older then they look. It is truly a miracle compound.

"It has given me superhuman strength and speed. It also gave me the ability to produce my own bullets when firing guns. I never run out of ammunition, ever, and I'm the fastest and most accurate marksman in the world. I can shoot high-speed moving objects, like bullets, tiny insects and far, fast-moving targets with superhuman accuracy and speed; that's why they call me Quick Shot. But I must warn you that the Rebel serum has its side-effects. It is extremely dangerous. Many men have lost their minds or died while being injected. The Faker was injected and he acquired very strange and unstable abilities. Only the strongest of minds can handle this injection, and I truly believe that you have what it takes; you can handle this."

The Black Skull says, "I'm not afraid. I will do it, and I will survive." So Quick Shot straps the Black Skull into the chair, and they inject the serum into his veins. The Rebel serum takes effect straight away. The Black Skull begins to scream as he feels its extreme pain, but 5 minutes later he calms down. They un-strap him and ask him, "Do you feel any different?" Black Skull looks at them, smiles and says, "Yes, the power I feel is indescribable." He then punches the concrete column beside him and breaks it in half, then the Black Skull looks at Quick Shot and tells him, "Shoot me 10 times."

Quick Shot replies, "But you will die." The Black Skull then says, "NO, no, I won't, just trust me." Quick Shot picks up his gun and starts firing directly at the Black Skull, then miraculously the Black Skull catches 9 out of the 10 bullets with his bare hands. The last bullet manages to hit him in the chest, but it bends and it does not affect him. Everyone in the room gets shocked and astonished. Then the Black Skull says, "Let 20 of the best men in this room attack me with everything they have." Twenty of the best men rush up and start attacking him. The Black

Skull evades all their attacks with superhuman speed and manages to drop all 20 men to the ground in less than 60 seconds. Quick Shot becomes extremely impressed and says, "What is this ability?" The Black Skull replies, "The Rebel serum made me become a super martial arts fighter, and I have become the best fighter in the world. It has given me superhuman strength, agility and speed. I can catch bullets and kill a thousand men if I desire." Quick Shot smiles and says, "This time they don't stand a chance; no one can stop us, but we must expand."

Black Skull then says, ''Before we can expand we must first protect our identities. We are fugitives on the run and we can't have police track us down so easily so three day's ago I visited an old friend and he will be here soon with our new high tech war plated armor and disguises especially designed by me for optimal performance and protection. One hour later the mask maker arrives and hands the Black Skull 10 boxes and 2 metal briefcases. The Black Skull then grabs the 2 briefcases and tells Quick Shot, "The mask maker and I have personally taken the liberty to design these especially for you." Black Skull then opens up the briefcases and hands Quick Shot a high-tech professionally designed full armor-plated suit with a metal bulletproof helmet, a metal pole, a sword, 2 handguns and a sniper.

The rest of the League of Desolation members open up the boxes and find many high-tech war plated armor, and bulletproof black skeleton masks.

The Black Skull then says, ''Suit up boys; you're all going to need these for what's about to come.''

Quick Shot and the Black Skull decide that they need more money to expand their operation, so they decide to rob the Central City gold bank.

Chapter 7: The mastermind criminal

One week later 3 police cars park outside the Central City gold bank, then the police quickly rush in and say, "We suspect that a robbery might occur at this time in this bank; please evacuate the perimeter and stay calm." The police then enter the back room and take all of the bank's staff members from behind the bulletproof glass and put them in a line next to the bank's customer waiting area. Then they take 5 customers and put them 20 feet away from them, while the police guard the bank door. The Black Skull and his crew suddenly rush in. The police quickly point their guns at them and catch them off guard. They outnumber them and put Black Skull and his crew on the ground. The police point their guns downwards at Black Skull and his crew for about 2 minutes. Then the police suddenly turn around and quickly shoot the 5 bank customers and all standing staff members, except for one , with silencer guns. All the shot staff members and the customers drop to the ground and die. The Black Skull then gets up and tells the police, "Good work, boys, just like we planned." (The cops who rushed into the bank were all paid by Black Skull. Some of them were fake cops and some were corrupt police looking for extra money. Black Skull set up this ingenious plan so no alarms would go off and no real cops would come into the bank and arrest him.) One of the fake police's phone radio comes on inside the bank and real police from a nearby area ask if they need any backup. The corrupt police officer replies and says, "No, everything is under control. The criminals are in custody and innocent bystanders are all safe." Then

Black Skull and some of his men head towards the vault that contains the gold. They pick up the last remaining bank worker and put a gun to his head and command him to open the vault, so he does, after the vault opens, the Black Skull picks up his gun and shoots the last remaining worker in the head. Then Black Skull and his men enter the vaulted room and what they see shocks them. They see a large room which is completely made of gold--the walls, the floors and the ceiling are completely made of gold, and there are piles and piles of stacked gold and golden statues everywhere. The Black Skull then laughs and says, "Oh, isn't this something? It's beautiful. We hit the jackpot, boys; we're going to be filthy rich. Upload the gold into the truck and let's go." Then his men upload the gold into the trucks, and they quickly head off.

Chapter 8: The abandoned warehouse

After the bank robbery, Black Skull and his crew return to their hideout, which is in an old, rundown, abandoned warehouse located far away from Central City. In the warehouse Black Skull and his men have a meeting in Black Skull's office. There the Black Skull congratulates his men, and then they begin counting the gold they stole (in the office there are exactly 11 men including Black Skull; and 2 out of the 11 men are wielding weapons). Moments, later 2 of Black Skull's men who were wielding the weapons get electrocuted and drop to the ground. By the Black Devil from above who is using a taser gun called the "Devil wave," which is a gun that delivers more than 400 volts of electricity, which knocks out enemies cold.

The Black Skull and his men look around to find who's shooting but they don't seem to find anyone because the Black Devil's suit contains high tech technology in it which allows it to camouflage with any surface. (The Black Devil is hiding in the concrete corner above the ceiling and because the Black Devil used his camouflage technology on his suit, he and the concrete became one; it looks like the concrete is firing at them.) Then one by one Black Skull's men get shocked and drop on the ground. The Black Devil then comes gliding down and says to Black Skull, "Who are you?"

The Black Skull replies, "You really don't know who I am? I'm Central City's most recognized and feared criminal, the king of the drug underworld, the one and only Black Skull, and the newest member of the League of Desolation, trained by the very men you wanted to destroy. I've been injected with the last dose of the Rebel serum and you've been injected with the devil serum— it's man against man and today; we will see who's more powerful. We go way back Mr. Jonathon . My name is John Michaels, and Dan Michaels was my beloved father and you killed him. Do you still remember that night when that broken–down, scared child was crying and begging you to spare his father's life? The child begged you but you would not listen--well, that child was me. I pleaded with you that night but you just killed him, right in front of me, and you left him lying in his own blood."

The Black Devil then says, "I did not mean to hurt you, but there are some things which you do not understand. Your father was an evil man. He killed hundreds of innocent people, including my family. I do not kill innocent people. I only hunt down the criminals and the oppressors."

The Black Skull angrily says, "YOU ARE A LIAR AND A COLD-BLOODED CRIMINAL. MY FATHER CHANGED HIS WAYS YEARS AGO; HE WAS A GOOD MAN, but you killed him and left me to rot on the streets of Central City. You were the one who made my life miserable, you are responsible for all the evil and pain in my life and you will pay dearly for all you have done. Razor was my master's brother, and you killed him too. You and this corrupt city have taken our family and our friends. My mother was the first to fall within Central City, then Razor, and finally my father followed, but we will soon have our revenge and no one will be able to stop the League of Desolation."

The Black Devil says, "But I thought the League of Desolation was dead. I thought I wiped all of them out completely after I killed your father."

The Black Skull smiles and says, "No, we survived and regrouped and we became much more powerful within the prisons, and now we are growing in numbers every day. Our destiny will not be denied."

Then suddenly one of Black Skull's men wakes up, grabs his gun and aims it towards the Black Devil, but before he could shoot, the Blue Eagle comes out of the shadows and takes him out cold. The Black Skull then rushes towards the Blue Eagle and starts attacking him. The Black Devil intervenes, then the Black Skull starts fighting the Black Devil and the Blue Eagle at the same time, and even though it's 2 against 1, the Black Skull gets the upper hand and wins all the exchanges because the Black Skull is truly a well-trained and powerful fighter. The Blue Eagle then moves back grabs his gun and starts shooting at the Black Skull. The Black Skull quickly evades the bullets, rushes up and kicks the Blue Eagle in the face with a spinning back kick to the face. He then grabs his gun and breaks it in half.

Black Skull's men begin waking up, then one of Black Skull's men who was wielding a weapon grabs his gun and starts firing directly at the Blue Eagle, the bullets hit the Blue Eagle but they don't affect him . The person firing shortly runs out of bullets and before he could reload, the Blue Eagle quickly rushes up and knocks him out. Now no one in the room has weapons; it's all even. The Blue Eagle pulls out his blue glowing metal stick, and the Black Devil pulls out his triton then the Black Devil and the Blue Eagle begin fighting Black Skull and the other 7 remaining men; they proceed to have the most epic, and most unique fight ever.

The 7 remaining men get taken out during the fight, then it's once again Black Skull vs. the Blue Eagle and the Black Devil. This time the Blue Eagle and the Black Devil manage to get the upper hand and they drop Black Skull to the ground but unfortunately, he lands next to a rocket launcher which was placed beside the table. He grabs the rocket launcher, aims it at the Black Devil and shoots him. The rocket head explodes and injures the Black Devil very badly but fails to completely penetrate the skin because the Black Devil was injected with the devil serum which gave him a super-human body, the Black Skull then aims the rocket launcher towards the Blue Eagle. He pulls the trigger but the rocket launcher does not fire because there was only one rocket head inside the launcher. The Black Skull then throws the rocket launcher away and rushes towards the Blue Eagle, and they begin to fight again; meanwhile, the Black Devil is injured and his bleeding very badly. He knows he must get out of there or he will soon die, so he uses his belt to signal for his devil plane.

The devil plane automatically arrives over the building and locates the Black Devil by using infrared technology, then the plane shoots a small hole through the rooftop and automatically sends down a blue energy ray, which grabs the Black Devil and pulls him upwards safely into the plane's cockpit, and he escapes via devil abduction technology. The Black Skull and the Blue Eagle continue fighting. Black Skull gets the upper hand and kicks the Blue Eagle out of the glass window; the glass breaks and the Black Skull thinks the Blue Eagle is about to fall to his death, but the Blue Eagle quickly releases his wings and glides away to safety. All of Black Skull's men later wake up and Black Skull tells them in a loud voice, "We need to evacuate and find a new hideout right now; let's go."

(The Blue Eagle is a superhuman who was born with superhuman abilities; he was born super strong, his bones and skin are more powerful than metal and he came out of the womb with sharp claws and wings attached to his back.)

Chapter 9: The inner demon

Now the Black Devil is shot and is badly bleeding so his unseen devil protectors inside the plane, remove his suit and rush him to the nearest hospital. Due to his injury the Black Devil goes into deep sleep on the hospital bed, and during his nap he has a dream.

In the dream the Black Devil is wearing his devil suit and he is in a place which is completely white, so he says to himself, *Where am I? I... I'm I dead. I must be dead. Is this heaven?* Then all of a sudden the scenario changes, and he finds himself at his Grand Canyon town, then the doors of his parents' house open and he, his mom, his dad and his brothers and sisters come out , then the Black Devil says in a loud voice, "Mom, Dad, take your kids and go; you need to get out of here. The League is coming--they're coming. The Red Devil, Damien Black, Quick Shot, Razor and Dan Michaels are coming. You're about to die and I won't be there to help you; please save yourselves." But no one hears him because he is like a ghost.

Then Dan Michaels and his son Black Skull (here Black Skull is a man and he has his mask on) come towards the Klyde family. Black Skull then tells his dad, "Come on, Dad, take their money. We're poor and homeless and we need to eat, and if they resist then kill them--kill them all. It's either us or them; it's the survival of the fittest." Then after hearing this, the ghost Black Devil starts screaming and saying to his family, "Run, you're about to get shot;

run, save yourselves. Then Dan Michaels fires and kills Jonathon Klyde's entire family. After seeing this the Black Devil falls to his knees and starts crying and says, "Nooooooo, no, no, not again; this can't be happening again." The Black Skull then looks at the Black Devil's ghost and says, "SHUT YOUR DAMN MOUTH. YOU and your filthy family DESERVE TO DIE." The Black Skull then shoots him in the chest.

The Black Devil falls backwards and he falls into a deep, fiery hole. He keeps falling and then he hits his back really hard and screams from the pain, then he climbs out and heads to his cattle ranch home. Now he is bleeding from his chest. He puts his hand on the wound to stop the bleeding and enters his cattle ranch home, shouting loudly, "Help me, please help me, I've been shot. Kazelle , where are you?' Then he hears a voice saying, "Come here, Jonathon." The Black Devil turns around and sees a huge mirror in his living room. He goes up to the mirror and he starts looking at his reflection, then he says to his reflection, "Did you say that?" his reflection replies, "Yes, Jonathon, it was me--the Black Devil." "But who are you?"

The reflection says, "Let me show you who I am," then the reflection starts changing. The Black Devil 's devil suit inside the reflection starts ripping, then his reflection starts transforms into a large, scary devil with horns and wings, then the Horned Devil comes out of the mirror, stands next to the Black Devil and says, "Don't be scared, Jonathon, I'm your alter-ego, your evil side, your darkness, your fears, your anxiety and your hatred. I'm the demon that lives within you. I'm pure evil and I was born when your father and your family died and you lost everything you ever loved. And ever since that day I've been a burden living within you, tearing you apart from the inside. I'm your complete opposite, Jonathon. They call you the Black Devil but you may refer to me as Horned Devil or the inner demon, and if you want to defeat the evil which lies within you, then you have to kill me." The Horned Devil then opens his wings and fire starts rushing out. The Black Devil feels the heat and quickly moves away The Horned Devil then rushes towards the Black Devil and strikes him with his large claws, the Black Devil ducks and kicks him away, the Horned Devil comes back and starts striking again, the Black Devil dodges the attacks and counters with some heavy blows. The Horned Devil gets angry then grabs hold of the Black Devil and throws him across the room into the glass and wooden cabinet. The Horned Devil then flies towards the Black Devil but the Black Devil quickly grabs 5 small bombs and throws them directly at the Horned Devil's face. The blast from the bombs injure and weaken the Horned Devil, so the Black Devil rushes towards him and starts punching and kicking him in the face. The Horned Devil gets angry and grabs the Black Devil from his neck; he then expands his claws and delivers a powerful strike to the Black Devil's face but before the claw attack could penetrate the Black Devil 's face, the Black Devil quickly grabs hold of the Horned Devil's hands and starts moving them away The Horned Devil tries extremely hard to puncture the Black Devil's face but fails to do so. The Black Devil then twists the Horned Devil's hands and kicks him away into and through the furniture and concrete wall. The Horned Devil begins to scream, so the Black Devil takes this chance and runs out of the cattle ranch home, he then looks at the full moon and he begins to develop wings he then jumps up and starts flying extremely fast upwards towards the moon.

After a short while he lands on the moon's surface, and he says to himself, *I think I've lost him*. Then the Black Devil hears a voice from behind saying, "NO JONATHON, I'm right behind you." The Black Devil looks back and sees the Horned Devil standing behind him, then the Horned Devil and the Black Devil begin to have an epic fight on the moon, but in the end the Black Devil discovers his inner power, grabs the Horned Devil and throws him straight into the sun.

Then suddenly the black space begins opening above him, and white light rays, begin engulfing the darkness, then the light fades and Jonathon Clyde begins looking up and he sees his entire family, wearing white cowboy clothes and hats, sitting on top of white horses who are standing on white sparkling clouds in the heavens above. After seeing this Jonathon Clyde begins crying out in joy, and starts saying, "Mum, Dad, and my brothers and sisters, is that really you? I have missed you all so much. Please come back to me. I can't live without you." Then a light ray drops towards Jonathon Clyde and the light begins taking him upwards towards his family above. After a while he reaches his family and they all embrace, then Jonathon Clyde's mother and father say, "We are all proud of you Jonathon, you have become the hero you were always destined to be. You have stopped many evil and helped many people. Never give up Jonathon; we love you son. It's your time now; you must stop the League before it's too late. Now go son, go; we are all fine; there is no need to worry about us." Then Jonathon begins saying in a saddened voice, "Please don't go, don't leave me again. I've missed you all so much." The family then starts fading away and says, "We all believe in you Jonathon and we'll always be right with you in spirit and heart."

The Black Devil then wakes up and says to his devil companion Kazelle and the rest of his devil friends (which only he can see; no one else can see these devils except him because he was born with this ability), "I just had a realistic dream where I faced my inner demon and I won. I also meet my entire family in what seemed like heaven. They were all ok and happy together. We embraced and they told me how proud they were of me and everything I have accomplished. Now I feel different. I feel more free, more calm and collected." Then Kazelle says, "That wasn't just a dream, Jonathon, it was an unconscious spiritual healing. You just faced and defeated your inner demon, an unknown powerful devil that has been inside you ever since you lost your family. Your burdens have been overcome and now you are truly free." Then Jonathon Klyde's wife and her son rush into the hospital room, crying. Jonathon Clyde's wife looks at him and says, "Honey, you're alive. I thought you weren't going to make it; you had me worried." His son says, "DAD, DAD, you're awake; you didn't die. The doctors said you weren't going to make it but I never believed them not even for one second. I knew you were going to pull through; you always pull through, Dad." Jonathon Klyde then says, "I'm so happy to see you guys. I would never leave you; you both mean everything to me. I will always pull through for you; now let's go home."

Chapter 10: A bloody shootout

During the fight between Black Skull, the Black Devil and the Blue Eagle, Quick Shot was not inside the abandoned warehouse because he was driving in the streets of Central City, heading to the graveyard where his brother Razor was buried. In the graveyard Quick Shot pays his respects to his dead brother Razor, then he enters his car and drives away, and as he is driving through the streets he suddenly drives into an unexpected and hidden police road blockade where the police officers are stopping random passengers in order to catch the recently escaped prisoners. Quick Shot starts panicking in his car, he looks back to see if he can escape backwards, but he realizes he can't because there is a huge truck and many other vehicles behind him, so he quickly takes his foot off the brakes, overtakes the cars in front of him and drives straight ahead at high speed.

The police shout, "Release the spikes; somebody is trying to escape," then suddenly, large spikes pop up from under the ground. Quick Shot sees them and quickly turns his car to the left curb. His car steers out of control, flips over and quickly slams straight into the front entrance of a large commercial office building. The car door opens and Quick Shot falls out of the driver's seat, drops to the ground, and lands inside the office building. His car catches fire and gets stuck in between the office building door, blocking the front and only entrance to the building. Injured and shaken, Quick Shot gets up and starts running up the stairs. Then all of a sudden Quick Shot's car blows up. The explosion from the blast ignites a large fire and the entire first and second levels of the building begin to burn.

Meanwhile, down below on the streets, police officers start calling for backup and within minutes firefighters and special task force police officers arrive and surround the entire office building. Meanwhile, above, Quick Shot finally reaches the rooftop. He opens the roof door and walks towards the balcony. He looks down below and sees a large number of police officers hiding behind shields and bulletproof cars, all aiming their guns upwards towards him. Then the head of police steps up with a large microphone and says in a loud voice, "Quick Shot, you're completely surrounded, so just put your weapons down and place your hands on top of your head, and one of our helicopters will come and escort you down safely."

Quick Shot replies, "Do you really think you can take me back to prison that easily? I will not surrender. Today it's either you die or I do."

The head of police then says, "Please don't do this. The building you're standing on is on fire and it will soon be completely engulfed with flames, and you're clearly outnumbered 80 men to 1; this will end very badly for you. If we fire you will die. This is your final warning: either surrender quietly or face the deadly consequences."

Quick Shot raises both of his guns in the air and says in a loud voice, "If you want me you have to kill me. I will never go down without a fight, and if I die today then I'm taking all of you with me."

The head of police then says to the police force, "All officers prepare to take immediate action. This man cannot be reasoned with; he is completely out of his mind."

One of the police officers says, "This man is crazy. What can he do with only two small handguns? He is going to get himself killed."

Then suddenly 5 police officers get taken out by a barrage of ultra-fast bullets. The rest of the police officers panic and take cover, then all of them begin to fire back at Quick Shot above. Hundreds of bullets race towards Quick Shot, so he takes action and fires back but he gets hit many times, so he decides to move sideways and take cover under the concrete balcony. Then the police commander says, "Hold your fire; I think we got him. I think he is dead. Let's move in. Let the fire trucks contain the blaze and send 2 helicopters up there and get him down."

At that point the entire police force let their guards down and the fire trucks move in and start spraying water at the fire-engulfed building, then all of a sudden Quick Shot gets back up and shoots the two fire trucks with 2 rounds of ultra-fast, deadly bullets. The fast bullets penetrate the trucks, which makes them blow up and flip over onto the police cars behind. The explosion and the shrapnel from the fire trucks' explosions hits and kills 10 officers. The rest of the police force panics and runs for cover. Quick Shot keeps firing at the police force with a barrage of ultra-fast, never-ending bullets, and with each passing minute more and more police begin die and their cars begin to blow up in their faces, sending shrapnel and shock waves across the entire area. The remaining 40 police officers desperately fight back and begin to fire at Quick Shot with everything they've got, and hundreds of bullets race towards Quick Shot. Quick Shot sees the bullets coming straight at him, so he quickly aims and shoots down all lethal incoming bullets with his gun. He even manages to split some of the police's bullets in half by using his superhuman hand speed and accuracy.

The police become extremely shocked and terrified quick then grabs his black sniper from his back strap and one by one, he starts sniping and shooting down almost all the police officers below. Only 7 survive and flee the scene, then 3 police helicopters arrive and hover above Quick Shot and begin to throw sleeping gas bombs on the rooftop. The dark sleeping gas spreads and Quick Shot begins to feel its effects, then one of the helicopters begins to shoot Quick Shot with a sniper rifle. Quick Shot rolls out of the way and shoots the helicopter with a barrage of bullets. The helicopter begins to break and it crashes to the ground. The other 2 helicopters begin to fire heavy duty bullets and throw an excessive amount of sleeping gas, tear gas and stun bombs. The deadly bombs take full effect and Quick Shot falls to the ground and faints, then one of helicopters lands on the rooftop. They handcuff Quick Shot and take him away. After a short trip the helicopters land and the police on the ground grab and take Quick Shot back to the police station and book him a court date. The word spreads and the newspapers publish the Quick Shot arrest story, and all the TV news stations broadcast the story live.

Over at the new hideout the Black Skull hears about the news and tells his men, "Everyone prepare yourselves; we're going to get Quick Shot."

Chapter 11: The cattle ranch

Two days later Jonathan Klyde gets cleared and he checks out of the hospital, then he and his family return to their cattle ranch home. At the ranch Jonathan takes care of his animals and spends some time with his family for a few days. A day later he decides to take his wife, his kid, and a few of his friend's horse riding and afternoon camping.

The next day Jonathon Klyde's family and his friends all gather together, ,they then get on their horses and head towards the campsite. After riding for a while they finally reach their destination and at the campsite they all build tents, talk, swim and have fun. A few hours later everyone gathers around the campfire and they all begin talking and having a great time, then all of a sudden everything around him becomes slower. The camp fire changes and Jonathon Klyde sees a scary vision of a large beast coming out of the fire, standing in front of him saying, "You think you're safe. I will kill you; you will not be able to help them. You're nothing to me. If the League can't stop you then I will. Be afraid, Jonathon. The darkness is coming." The large beast keeps making threats in a loud voice. The fire starts surrounding Jonathon Klyde. His face starts changing color and he starts finding it hard to breathe, speak or move, then the beast screams one last time, "You are not safe. Fear me; fear the darkness."

Then Jonathon Klyde pops back to reality and faints. His friends pick him up and take him back home, then 2 hours later he wakes up in his bed and tells his family and friends what has just happened to him, but the next day life continues as normal.

Chapter 12: The courthouse hearing

Approximately one week later Quick Shot gets taken out of prison by the police officers, who then place him inside a police car and take him to his court hearing. Quick Shot enters the courthouse and sits down and another pair of handcuffs are placed on both his hands and legs, then a judge named Alex enters the courtroom and sits down. Alex and Quick Shot begin to speak, and exactly 1 hour into Quick Shot's court hearing, five black vans surround the courthouse. The doors of the black vans open up and Black Skull and 30 of his men get out and rush into the courthouse.

Black Skull then opens the courthouse door and says in a loud voice, "NOBODY MOVE. WE ARE ABOUT TO TAKE ALL YOU PEOPLE AS HOSTAGES AND IF ANYONE TRIES TO RUN AWAY OR FIGHT BACK, WE WILL KILL THEM." Black Skull's men point their guns towards everyone inside the courthouse and they also surround the entire courtroom from the inside and outside, then Black Skull calls the authorities and tells them, "We have taken everyone in this courthouse as hostages, and if you don't follow my requests exactly, all these people here will suffer horribly. First, no one should come near us or near this courthouse; if we see just 1 police officer or 1 news reporter nearby, we will kill all the hostages. Second, when we finish our business here and try to get away, let no one follow us because we will be taking 4 hostages with us, and if you follow us or get anywhere near us we will kill the hostages but if you don't follow us and leave us alone we will drop the hostages off in a safe place so they can return home safely."

The authorities agree to his requests, he then shuts the phone off and looks at the judge, and he sees the same judge that sentenced him to life in prison. Black Skull then walks towards the judge and says, "MR. ALEX, DO YOU REMEMBER ME? I'm the drug lord you sent to prison 6 years ago and before I went out of the courtroom that day I told you that you were a dead man, and I did not lie; I'm a man of my words." Alex the judge says, "No, please don't hurt me; I have a wife and 2 kids at home. Please, I'm begging you." Black Skull says, "Shut your mouth, keep calm, and I may consider sparing your miserable life." The Black Skull then walks up to the security guard and takes his handcuff keys which are strapped to his belt, Black Skull then walks towards Quick Shot and unlocks all his handcuffs and says to all his men in a loud voice, "Let's get out of here; take 4 hostages with you and let's go."

Black Skull, Quick Shot and the rest of their men all head toward the courthouse door, but just before leaving, Black Skull turns around looks directly at Alex the judge and says in a loud voice, "I told you you were a dead man and I'm a man of my word, so here you go." Black Skull then quickly pulls out his handgun and shoots Alex 3 times in the chest. Alex the judge drops to the ground and dies, then Black Skull, Quick Shot and the rest of their men all run out and get into their black vans and leave.

Chapter 13: The blazing fire

Shortly after Black Skull, Quick Shot and the rest of their men enter their new compound; The Black Skull then says, "Welcome back" and gives Quick Shot a brand new high-tech professionally designed full armor-plated suit with a metal bulletproof helmet, a sword, and 2 handguns. He then tells Quick Shot, "There's a small shipment of drugs coming from Cuba. Can you take some men and pick up the drugs?" Quick Shot then tells his men, "Let's go," and they all leave.

Very late at night Quick Shot and his men arrive at the location on the beach, then the Cuban ship arrives near the shore. The Cuban comes out and says, "Where do you want me to put the drugs?" Quick Shot tells his men, "Upload the drugs into the vans and drive back to the compound. I'll follow you after a bit; I just have to pay and talk to the Cuban first." So Quick Shot's men begin uploading the drugs into their vans. But what Quick Shot and his men don't know is that the Black Devil secretly followed them and he is now nearby. He is camouflaged and he is listening and watching their every move from above. After Quick Shot's men upload all the drugs into the van they drive off and leave, then Quick Shot enters the ship and goes inside to speak to the Cuban.

The Black Devil takes out a gun and shoots a tiny microchip from above into the cabin room door where Quick Shot and the Cuban are located. He aims the listening device towards the boat's cabin room and listens to the conversation between the Cuban and Quick Shot.

Shortly afterward Quick Shot pays the Cuban his money and leaves, but as Quick Shot is leaving he notices a tiny chip on the boat's door. He takes the tiny chip off the door and crushes it, looks around and says to the Cuban in a loud voice, "WELL, IT LOOKS LIKE WE'RE BEING WATCHED BY THE DEVIL." The Cuban says, "Who's the devil?" Quick Shot replies, "THE BLACK DEVIL." Then Quick Shot goes to the middle of the boat and says, "BLACK DEVIL, STOP YOUR HIDING, YOU COWARD; COME OUT FROM THE SHADOWS AND FACE ME LIKE A REAL MAN." The Black Devil hears him and comes gliding down onto the boat, where he comes face-to-face with Quick Shot.

Quick Shot says, "Speak of the devil and he shall appear." The Black Devil then says, "I have called the police and they will be here any minute now." Quick Shot and the Cuban then start hearing loud police sirens coming from a distance. The Cuban panics and says, "NO WAY, MAN, IM NOT GOING BACK TO JAIL. I'M GETTING THE HELL OUT OF HERE RIGHT NOW." The Cuban rushes to the ship's steering wheel and puts the paddle on full speed. The Black Devil is now stuck about to fight Quick Shot on a speeding boat heading for Cuba.

While the boat is moving at full speed, Quick Shot tells the Black Devil, "IT'S BEEN A LONG TIME, MR. JONATHON. FIRST YOU BURN OUR COMPOUND TO THE GROUND THEN YOU KILL OUR LEADERS AND MASTERS, ALJABAAR LUCIFER AND HIS

SON DAMIAN BLACK. YOU DISRESPECTED US FOR FAR TOO LONG AND MOST RECENTLY YOU KILLED MY DEAR FRIEND DAN MICHAELS AND MY BROTHER RAZOR. YOU HUNT US DOWN LIKE ANIMALS AND DESTROY EVERYTHING OUR GREAT LEADERS AND GOVERNMENT HAVE EVER WORKED FOR. BUT YOU WILL PAY FOR WHAT YOU HAVE DONE, AND THAT I GUARANTEE."

THE BLACK DEVIL THEN SAYS, "I had to do what was right; you, your brother and the rest of the League of Desolation members were nothing but evil PSYCHOPATHS. You and they slaughtered my family and half my town, and the League was going to destroy Central City and the world, killing thousands of innocent people THAT DID NOT DESERVE TO DIE. Quick Shot says, "No, the League of Desolation was going to liberate the world and cast out the criminals and the corrupt, but you just don't seem to understand. Today is the day you die. We will have our revenge and fulfill our destiny. This city and the rest of the world will be ours very soon; we simply cannot be denied." Quick Shot takes out his sword, then tells the Black Devil, "Let's see how well the devils have taught you."

The Black Devil pulls out a small sized piece of metal. He presses a button, then the piece of metal expands and becomes a metal spear with 3 sharp knives attached to the end of it, which can fire powerful red energy rays when fired. The Black Devil then says, "You will pay for murdering my family and the rest of my town. Today I want to watch you suffer just like you made us suffer."

Quick Shot then rushes up to the Black Devil, and they start having an intense sword fight. During the fight they knock down two barrels containing petrol. The petrol spills all around the boat. Then the Black Devil moves back and starts throwing electric spearheads at Quick Shot, but Quick Shot reacts and manages to deflect all the spearheads away from his body by using his sword. The Black Devil tries again and throws 4 more spearheads. Quick Shot panics, takes out his gun and shoots them all, deflecting them away from him once again, but unfortunately this time the electric spearheads land on the spilled petrol and the electricity from the spearheads ignite a huge flame, setting the entire boat on fire. Even though there's a huge fire on the boat, Quick Shot and the Black Devil continue on fighting, and during the fight Quick Shot gains the upper hand, attacks the Black Devil and kicks him straight into the massive fire.

The Black Devil covers his face and his body with his fireproof cape, then he quickly comes out from the blazing fire. Quick Shot sees him and strikes the Black Devil with his sword. The Black Devil blocks it and Quick Shot's sword gets stuck in the Black Devil 's three-headed devil spear (aka the devil's triton). The Black Devil then does a quick arm twist and breaks Quick Shot's sword in half. Now Quick Shot has no sword, so the Black Devil uses this opportunity and starts viciously attacking Quick Shot with his 3-headed spear, hoping he will finally kill him, but Quick Shot keeps moving back and side to side, avoiding all of the Black Devil's triton attacks. The Black Devil strikes again but Quick Shot grabs his 3-headed spear and kicks him away. Then Quick Shot pulls out his 2 handguns and starts shooting the Black Devil. While shooting, Quick Shot manages to hit the Black Devil many times, pushing him backwards and injuring him badly with ultra–fast, deadly bullets.

The Black Devil begins to panic and runs away. He starts moving and running around the boat, seeking cover from the barrage of bullets, but unfortunately he fails to find any relief. Quick Shot keeps on chasing and shooting the Black Devil with many rounds of never-ending bullets, which push the Black Devil back and launches him into the boat's hard cargo. Then the Black Devil changes his tactics and tries something new. He begins to jump out of the way, but eventually he lands in the corner, where he gets himself stuck.

While stuck in the corner Quick Shot manages to hit the Black Devil with 100 rounds of super-fast bullets every 3 seconds. The Black Devil tries to escape the barrage of fast bullets but fails to do so. Every time he gets hit with a hundred rounds of bullets he flies backwards and hits the ship's hard exterior, then collapses on the ground. Then he tries to get back up again and every time he tries to get back up on his feet the same thing happens, so the Black Devil desperately decides to change his tactics or else he will die. The third time the Black Devil hits the ground, he grabs a time bomb from his belt, and as he is getting up he quickly throws the time bomb in the air, which makes Quick Shot and his bullets travel in slow motion. The Black Devil knows that the effects of the time bomb won't last long so he takes his opportunity, grabs his devil staff and uses it to fire 2 energy rays at Quick Shot's hands, which makes Quick Shot's guns fly into the water. The Black Devil then drops to his knees and as the effects of the time bomb wear off, Quick Shot rushes up to the Black Devil. The Black Devil gets up and strikes Quick Shot with his devil's staff. Quick Shot blocks the attack, and breaks the Black Devil's triton in half.

Now the Black Devil and Quick Shot are both without weapons on a boat with a huge fire travelling at full speed to Cuba, and it's in the middle of the night, and the boat is in danger of blowing up any minute, but because of the hatred they have for each other, they ignore all signs of obvious danger and continue on fighting. During the fight they exchange many punches and heavy blows. But both of them know that the boat is in danger of blowing up any minute now, so Quick Shot pushes the Black Devil away. He then calls up Black Skull by pressing a tiny button located on his helmet. Black Skull picks up, then Quick Shot says, "Black Skull, you need to come get me. I'm in the middle of the ocean and I'm trouble."

Black Skull then tells his men, "I put a chip inside his suit. Mark his location and go get him. HURRY UP." The Black Devil and Quick Shot continue fighting and during the fight Quick Shot becomes very aggressive and relentlessly starts offloading with heavy punches and kicks; he then grabs the Black Devil and launches through a hot burning metal container. The Black Devil gets seriously injured and burned. He becomes angry and his anger reaches the boiling point. His blood starts rushing and he starts transforming, so he grabs some smoke bombs from his belt and throws them on the ship's floor, then the

Black Devil starts running towards the back of ship and jumps straight into the massive blazing fire. Quick Shot's vision becomes blurred because of all the smoke and fire, then Quick Shot hears a loud noise coming from the back of the ship. He looks and sees a huge red devil with black horns and wings coming out of the black, smoky red fire. Quick Shot becomes extremely terrified and says in a loud voice, "NO, HE HAS transformed INTO THE FORSAKEN DEMON; THERES NO STOPING HIM NOW." Panicked and scared, Quick Shot turns around and starts running towards the boat's cabin room.

The transformed Black Devil flies after him and tries to grab him, but Quick Shot quickly jumps through the cabin room and shuts the metal door. The transformed Black Devil flies and hits the metal door face-first, then a second later a barrel filled with petrol located next to him explodes and blows up in his face. The explosion from the petrol blast injures the transformed Black Devil badly and launches him 40 meters into the air. The transformed Black Devil becomes extremely angry. He flies downwards and grabs the boat from underneath, then with all his power he picks up and flips the boat, slamming it upside down into the water. The transformed Black Devil then flies away and heads back to Central City.

Inside the upside-down boat, water starts pouring into the cabin room. Quick Shot opens the metal door and tells the Cuban, "Come on, we need to get out of here; this boat is about to explode and sink." Quick Shot and the Cuban get out of the cabin door and swim forward beneath the ocean surface, away from the burning boat. Then they float to the surface, and 30 seconds later the boat blows up and sinks. Twenty minutes later, Black Skull's men come and rescue Quick Shot and the Cuban.

Chapter 14: The eagle attacks

Straight after the boat incident Black Skull and Quick Shot come to the conclusion that the police force might give them trouble so they decide to weaken Central City police by attacking the police force when they least expect it. At 4:00 in the morning Black Skull and his men invade more than 10 police stations; there they break the windows and doors, kill hundreds of cops and take their cars and uniforms. During the invasions Black Skull and his men prove to be too much for the police force because of their superior high-tech weaponry.

Black Skull told his men to find the investigation paperwork of his dad's murder and to erase all other evidence of his criminal activities, pictures and everything. So Black Skull's men do as they're told and gather all the evidence, delete the files on the computers and burn all pictures and paperwork. After Black Skull's men successfully invade the police stations they begin to leave and head towards their cars. (There are about 12 cars.)

Meanwhile the Blue Eagle is standing on top of a building located beside the police station waiting for them and as Black Skull's men come rushing out of the police station, they quickly get into their cars but before they could drive away the wheels of 2 cars get shot by the Blue Eagle above. After seeing this Black Skull's men quickly turn their car's ignition on and drive away. The Blue Eagle spreads his blue wings and jumps off the building, he then starts chasing them, gliding from 1 building to the other in order to catch up with all the fast moving cars. He keeps gliding in the air and shooting the wheels of the moving cars with his sniper until he gets 8 of the ten cars. And Every time the blue eagle would shoot their wheels, the cars of Black Skull's men would either spin out of control, crash or flip over, which would force Black Skull's men to get out of their vehicles and make a run for it on foot, and as the men run on the streets of Central City, the Blue Eagle would fly after them from above the rooftops, then he would start tracking, locating and shooting all the men with tranquilizers from above. The other men start shooting back at the Blue Eagle, who is flying in the sky near the high rooftops above them, hoping they will kill him, but every time they would shoot their bullets would miss, because the Blue Eagle would see their bullets coming and he would quickly move out of the way, miraculously dodging everything with extreme speed and skill. The men continue on shooting but the Blue Eagle keeps on moving and shooting them back until he eventually tranquilizes 90% of them, then the Blue Eagle looks around from above and sees that there is one man left standing below.

The man looks at the Blue Eagle and starts firing. The Blue Eagle moves out of the way then quickly flies downwards toward the final man. The man on the ground panics and tries to run away but the Blue Eagle snatches him up (just like an eagle snatches his prey) and slams him into the car, the Blue Eagle then grabs the man and says in a loud voice, "WHO ARE YOU WORKING FOR, WHO ORDERED YOU TO INVADE THE POLICE STATIONS AND WHY?" The man replies in a panicked voice, "Nobody, nobody sent us; we work for no one. We're just a bunch of criminals. Honestly, we work for nobody." The Blue Eagle gets angry and says in a loud voice, "YOU'RE LYING." The Blue Eagle grabs the man by his shirt and flies with him upwards towards the open sky. The man begins screaming, then high above the city the Blue Eagle stops in midair and tells the man in a loud voice, "I WILL ASK YOU AGAIN AND IF YOU DON'T TELL ME WHO SENT YOU, I WILL DROP YOU." The man starts panicking and says, "PLEASE DON'T DO THIS, PLEASE--I BEG YOU. IF I TELL YOU HIS NAME HE'LL TORTURE ME AND KILL MY FAMILY." The Blue Eagle then says, "I DON'T CARE. NOW I'M GOING TO COUNT TO 3 AND IF YOU DON'T TELL ME WHO SENT YOU AND WHERE I CAN FIND HIM I WILL DROP YOU AND YOU WILL DIE." The Blue Eagle starts counting, "One…" The man starts saying, "No, please, you don't understand; these men are not to be messed with." Blue Eagle then says, "Two" but before the Blue Eagle can say three, out of fear of exposing the League of Desolation, the man pulls out a small gun from behind his back and shoots himself in the head. Caught off guard, the Blue Eagle drops the man's dead body, then chases after him and grabs him. He then places him on the side of the street and flies away before real police come. Once the police arrive they arrest all the unconscious men and take them away for questioning. They also tow away all the broken cars and take the last man's dead body away for burial.

One day after the incident the town's mayor locates and contacts the Black Devil and he tells him to meet him on the rooftop of his office. There the Black Devil and the mayor talk about the Black Skull and his criminal activity. They also talk about the Blue Eagle.

The Black Devil says, "Put Black Skull back in prison; he's a fugitive on the run."

The mayor then says, "We can't; he erased all evidence of him ever being a criminal. He has nothing--no assault charges, no bank robberies, no prison breaks—NOTHING. You've really got your hands full this time. You might need some help."

The Black Devil asks, "Who's going to help me?"

The mayor replies, "I hate to admit it but Central City has a new protector. The Blue Eagle is back. I heard he has changed his ways; he now protects people from rooftops, gliding in the sky like a furious eagle, ready to attack when evil strikes. He can really help you put an end to this whole League of Desolation crisis. But you must keep him hidden; if the government ever finds him they will kill him."

The Black Devil says, "Jake, he is still a major wanted criminal. He and I had an all-out vicious fight awhile ago, but he did save my life when I was fighting the Black Skull in the warehouse, so maybe he has changed his ways, and you're right, I do need all the extra help I can get. I can't do this alone. I'll look into it, and I'll find him."

Chapter 15: The mass recruitment

Meanwhile Quick Shot and Black Skull want to create a massive civil war within America so they start posting propaganda videos online and they start having many secret underground meetings where they would recruit fed-up civilians who have had enough of the government's corrupt system into the League of Desolation.

Inside all the secret meetings the League of Desolation would give all the civilians weapons and tell them, "We will soon rise up and overtake this corrupt government. No one will be able to stand in our way. The League of Desolation is growing and we will continue growing until we become unstoppable. No one can stop us; no one will deny our destiny. When the time comes you're either with us or against us. When we say it's time to rise, all of you brave warriors grab your weapons and come out to the streets of Central City and help us fight the enemy. Then, after it's all over, we will give you everything you have ever desired and more."

The underground recruitment campaign gains popularity and soon the League of Desolation members grows into the millions.

Chapter 16: The secret lab

Shortly afterward the Black Devil gets into his plane and heads towards his secret high-tech laboratory located inside the mountains of the Grand Canyon. When the Black Devil reaches his destination, he presses the scan button and a secret entrance within the mountain high above opens up. He flies through the secret mountain entrance and he lands his plane inside the mountain. Inside his Grand Canyon mountain laboratory he finds 7 of his inter-dimensional devil friends waiting to speak to him inside the mountain cave. One of the devils says, "You're late, my friend; what took you so long?" The Black Devil replies, "Sorry about that, I have had a long week." Then another devil asks him, "So how have you been? We hear Central City is under attack by the League of Desolation, but how can that be? We thought the League was dead." The Black Devil says, "Yes, what you have heard is true. The League is back, and this is the reason I called you all here."

Then he and the rest of his inter-dimensional devil friends try to investigate and research about the Black Skull and Quick Shot. They search about their origin, their criminal activities and their life in prison. After doing some research the Black Devil and the rest of the devils find out that Black Skull is the son of Dan Michaels. They already knew that so they continue researching and find out that Black Skull is the most wanted criminal, with the largest organization of drug trafficking in Central City, and they also find out that he was trained by Aljabaar

Lucifer 's men inside the Central City prison and now the Black Skull, Quick Shot and the rest of the modern League of Desolation members want to create civil wars and take down all the governments of the world in order to fulfill their dream of becoming the sole and unmatched leaders of the world. They also find out how Black Skull is managing to gather so much high-tech weaponry, which he is planning to use to create an all-out civil war against Central City and the United States. After further research the Black Devil and the rest of the devils discover that Black Skull is receiving cheap and free of charge weapons from one of the biggest governmental gun companies in Russia, and the leader of this gun company is a man named Victor Lodge. Victor is affiliated with the Russian government and he is secretly trying to destroy America. He gives cheap and free of charge weapons to gangsters and watches Central City destroy itself out of revenge for what America did in WWI and WWII. Many of Victor's family and friends were killed during the war. Jonathon Klyde also finds out that Victor can't be arrested in Russia because he is related to the Russian vice president and in order to bring him to justice and stop his illegal importation of weapons, Jonathon Klyde must bring Victor back to Central City, where he can face trial.

Chapter 17: The journey to Russia

Jonathon Klyde decides to travel to Russia and arrest Victor Lodge at his palace, called the Winter Palace which is located in Saint Petersburg Russia. He asks the government for help and they provide him with a medium-sized modern warplane which can't be detected by radar.

The Black Devil then tracks and finds the Blue Eagle in order to try to convince him to come along. He comes face to face with the Blue Eagle; the Blue Eagle becomes anxious and gets ready to attack.

The Black Devil says in a loud voice, "Wait, hold on, I'm not here to fight or arrest you. I just want to talk. I really need your help."

The Blue Eagle says, "Oh yeah, and why should I trust you? You attacked me and tried to take me in for execution."

The Black Devil then says, "I know we have had our differences in the past but if you don't trust and help me, this entire city and the world is doomed. The League of Desolation has grown by millions and Quick Shot and Black Skull are planning to create an all-out civil war in both Central City and America, and if they succeed in the civil war they will then slowly but surely invade the entire world afterwards. We cannot allow that to happen. The government has given me a war plane and I'm going to Russia to arrest Victor, the man who's been supplying weapons to Black Skull and his men."

The Blue Eagle says, "I agree with you, but I can't deal with the government. I'm still an extremely wanted criminal and they want me dead."

The Black Devil says, "Don't worry, I will keep you a secret and hide you from them; they won't even know you're there."

The Blue Eagle then says, "Fine, I'll come with you but that's only because it is my duty and sole purpose to stop criminals like Quick Shot, Black Skull and their thugs and I need to stop this civil war from ever happening."

The Black Devil says, "Ok, but I must ask--you disappeared a couple of weeks back after our fight. Where did you go?"

"Honestly, I was just tired of everything--tired of people coming after me and tired of being wanted by the government--so I decided to travel far away from all the madness and spend my life off the grid with a group of likeminded people in the open forest, high above in the mountain tops, but then I heard these people called the League of Desolation came to Central City and they wanted to bring terror and oppression to innocent people. I couldn't just sit back and do nothing, so I had to come back and try to stop them, before it was too late. "

The Black Devil then tells the Blue Eagle to meet him in this specific location and he'll pick him up in 3 days.

The Blue Eagle agrees and three days later the Black Devil arrives at a remote location flying the war plane. He picks up the Blue Eagle, then both the Black Devil and the Blue Eagle enter the government aircraft and they embark on their journey to Russia. After traveling for 9 hours, they enter the snowy borders of Ukraine. The Ukrainian military border base locates a plane on their radar and thinks that the Black Devil's plane is a spy destroyer plane that Russia has sent to Ukraine for spying and destroying purposes, so the Ukrainian military base talk and decide they don't want to shoot the plane down using heavy weaponry, because they want to bring it down safely and study its technology. So they decide to send air force agents to bring it down from above safely.

A few minutes later a plane flies above the Black Devil's governmental aircraft, then 8 Ukrainian air force agents come abseiling down, break the windows and enter the plane, where they come face-to-face with the Black Devil. (The Black Devil has a very long rope which he was going to use, strapped to his body.) The Black Devil then looks at the 8 air force agents and tells the Blue Eagle in a loud, panicked voice, "OPEN THE PLANE DOOR; THE MILITARY AGENTS ARE HERE. THEY HAVE ENTERED THE AIRCRAFT." After hearing this the Blue Eagle presses the button and the large back door of the aircraft opens up, then the Black Devil jumps out of the plane and 6 of the 8 Ukrainian air force agents jump after him. The other 2 Ukrainian air force agents remain in the plane, in order to kill the Blue Eagle, hijack the controls and bring down the plane safely.

The agents rush up, and the Blue Eagle sees them coming so he quickly tries to put the plane on autopilot, but he fails to do so because his arm gets shot, so he quickly grabs his gun and moves out of the way. Now there is nobody controlling the plane steering wheel, and the autopilot is off, so the plane begins to free fall downwards rapidly. Zero gravity takes over and the 2 air force agents plus the Blue Eagle begin to float in similar conditions to outer space, then they began to fight in the zero gravity, the air force agents begin floating and firing at the Blue Eagle. The Blue Eagle gets shot and slams into the plane's interior. The agents shoot again but the Blue Eagle quickly moves to the side, and flies towards them. He then starts punching, kicking and seriously injuring the air force agents but eventually the force and the outward air pressure from the opened back door of the plane become too powerful and suck the Blue Eagle and the 2 agents straight out into the open air. The Blue Eagle uses his wings to keep him afloat, but the other 2 agents open their parachutes and begin to land safely.

Then the Blue Eagle looks downwards and sees his military plane falling at a rapid rate and it's about to crash in approximately 50 seconds. The Blue Eagle knows that their plane is their only ticket back home and if it crashes they will fail their mission of arresting Victor Lodge and stopping the civil war and then after the plane crashes they will be stuck on the ground fighting and eventually getting arrested by the Ukrainian military base, so adrenalin starts rushing into his veins. He focuses on the plane, spreads his wings and takes off he then starts chasing the plane downwards like a speeding rocket, and because of his ultra-fast speed and determination he eventually reaches the plane. He screams and flies towards the steering wheel, then he grabs the steering wheel and pulls the plane upwards, just seconds before crashing.

Meanwhile the Black Devil and the 6 Ukrainian air force agents that jumped out of the plane are now all free falling in the open air, and in the sky the air force agents begin to fire bullets and chase the Black Devil. In order to survive the Black Devil releases his grappling rope gun. He then fires it and it attaches to one of the air force agents. The grappling rope automatically pulls the Black Devil towards the attached agent, then the Black Devil quickly elbows him to the chin and knocks him out cold. The Black Devil then ties his long rope to the agent's parachute cord handle, then the Black Devil fights the remaining 5 agents one by one in the air. He kicks off the first agent and launches himself towards the second air force agent; the second air force agent and the black devil begin to fight in the midair but the Black Devil eventually knocks him out and ties his long rope to the agent's cord which is responsible for opening the parachute, then the Black Devil quickly pushes himself off the second agent and launches himself towards the third agent, where the same thing happens. In the end the black devil knocks out all the air force agents and ties his rope to all their parachute cord handles, he then flies upwards and pulls on his rope, which releases all the agents' parachutes at once. (Because the Ukrainian agents were all knocked out, the Black Devil couldn't let them fall to their death; that's why he was tying his rope to all their parachute cord handles, so he could release their parachutes and allow all of them to land safely.) The Black Devil then pulls his own parachute cord and lands on the ground near the Ukrainian border.

The Blue Eagle picks the Black Devil up and they continue their flight to Russia. After a while they arrive at the snowy borders of Russia. Inside the plane the Black Devil and the Blue Eagle look at a map and see that between the Winter Palace and the city there's a large river. The Black Devil tells the Blue Eagle to go to a remote area so he can reach the palace undetected, so the Blue Eagle goes to a remote area, and the Black Devil skydives to the ground. On the ground the Black Devil takes off his suit and puts it in his bag, he then walks a while and hitchhikes a ride to the Russian city. In the city he travels to the guarded river of the Winter Palace, he then changes back into his devil suit, puts on his scuba diving gear, and jumps into the large river; then he starts swimming towards Victor's compound and under the water he sees and enters the Winter Palace's piping systems. Then he comes out from a drain located on the premises of the Winter Palace. At the palace he quietly sneaks through the window and silently knocks out %80 of the guards by using little metal spearheads to the necks, sleeping smoke bombs and a silent version of the "devil wave gun." He goes through the whole facility without being detected. He then reaches Victor's room, and before Victor could call for help, the Black Devil shoots his mouth with commercial glue. He then grabs and injects Victor with a needle filled with a sleeping agent, which makes Victor go to sleep. The Black Devil then silently cuts open one of the windows, shoots a zip line, and he and Victor Lodge zip line to a nearby building. Guards later enter Victor's room to check on him but find that Victor is missing. (In this scene it's snowing in Russia and in the Ukraine.)

Victor Lodge is then taken back to America and the Black Devil hands him over to the American government, where he faces trial. Ten days later the Russian government contacts the American government and tells them that they will stop importing illegal weapons to America under one condition: they will have to release Victor Lodge and drop all charges. The American government agrees, and Victor Lodge gets taken back to Russia.

Chapter 18: Street wars, a complex situation

Outraged by the news of Victor's arrest, Black Skull and the leaders of the League of Desolation decide to shoot up Central City while driving and create war. The next day the Black Skull, Quick Shot and the rest of the League of Desolation members sit on the windows of their cars and start driving towards Central City. On the streets of Central City they start drive-by shooting buildings, houses, banks, and shops, killing and injuring hundreds of people.

Meanwhile, on the streets you see normal police walking, minding their own business, then all of sudden things get out of control and the normal police become crazy and they start attacking and shooting other police offers and innocent civilians for absolutely no apparent reason. And farther downtown other police officers also start shooting and killing innocent people on the streets, and inside the police stations cops begin locking up other police officers inside their own prison cells. After seeing this, the people begin to panic and run away because they can't trust anyone anymore.

The shooting continues, then the Black Devil comes to the scene driving his hovering futuristic motorbike, which can travel up any surface like buildings and steep mountains. The Black Devil looks around at the all the chaos and sees some cops shooting innocent people. The Black Devil gets off his bike and starts attacking the fake and corrupt cops, then real and uncorrupt cops come driving by and see the Black Devil attacking the uniform-wearing police. The real cops think that the Black Devil is attacking police officers so they start shooting at him (unaware that the Black Devil is really attacking Black Skull's men, who are wearing fake police uniforms), but the Black Devil manages to get away and drives his bike across the streets of Central City, trying to solve the complex situation.

He then looks upwards and sees fake police officers on top of a high rise building sniping innocent people below, so the Black Devil turns his bike around and drives his bike up the high rise building at full speed. The fake police officers see the Black Devil's motorbike driving up the building and heading towards them, so they grab their snipers and rocket launchers and start shooting at him, but every time they would shoot their bullets and rocket heads would miss, because the Black Devil would see their bullets coming and he would quickly move out of the way, miraculously dodging everything with extreme speed and skill. The men continue shooting but the Black Devil keeps on moving and shooting them back with his motorcycle guns until he eventually kills 6 out of the 10 men. He then reaches the rooftop, and jumps off his bike, where he fights and finishes off the 4 remaining men. He then gets on top of the balcony and starts scanning for Black Skull.

Meanwhile, on the street the real police find Black Skull and shoot him in the shoulder 3 times, then they take him back to the police station for interrogation, only to find that he is a fake. They take his mask off and find out he is not John Michaels but rather an imposter pretending to be the Black Skull. The police later find 3 other Black Skull imposters as well. The real Black Skull drives to Jonathon Klyde's aka the Black Devil's cattle ranch home and at the cattle ranch home Black Skull finds Jonathan Klyde's wife and her family and the mayor and his family hiding out. They knock both of them to the ground and kidnap them. (The Black Skull couldn't find Jonathon Klyde's son because his son had run away and was hiding in the basement.) Then Black Skull and his men drive away. The Black Devil comes and starts following them. The Black Skull comes out of the passenger window and shoots the Black Devil's bike with a heavy high-tech rocket launcher. The Black Devil's bike catches fire, breaks and becomes unusable. The Black Devil falls off his bike and lands next to a group of police officers who are riding riot control horses. He gets on one of the horses, then he and the rest of the police officers start chasing Black Skull and his crew. Cops control the horses with one hand and shoot with the other hand. Black Skull and his crew start shooting back and 2 cops and the Black Devil get shot and knocked off their horses and 3 of Black Skull's men die during the chase. But Black Skull manages to get away.

Chapter 19: the military bases

In order to create a massive civil war in Central City Black Skull needs more weapons, which his organization is running really low on because of Victor Lodge's arrest. So he decides to steal from the military. He announces that he will be stealing from the government on national TV. The next day at 5:30pm the League of Desolation hack into the TV news channels, then the Black Skull shows up on national TV and says to the people, "Central City is a place of corruption, where people like the police and the Black Devil claim to help people and protect lives, but in reality they only kill and oppress. Central City is where drugs are being used on daily basis. It is a place of crime and corruption. We will fulfill our destiny and finally conquer Central City along with the world. Eventually Central City will burn to the ground, but first we need more weapons to start our civil war so we will be stealing weapons from Central City's eastern military base in exactly 5 days." After the announcement the government prepares for his coming

Five days later Black Skull sends his men to steal from the military base. Some of his men get into and drive police cars while others drive normal cars. While Black Skull's men are driving, suddenly they see the Black Devil's hovering car driving behind them. They start shooting at him with guns. The Black Devil shoots back and hits the wheels of the two cars driving in front him, which makes the two cars spin out of control and crash, then the Black Devil speeds up and hits another car from the side. He then drives between 2 cars, 1 car to his left and 1 car to his right. He puts his hovering car on autopilot, then he releases a mini screen next to the passenger seat which allows him to see the sides of the 2 cars. He presses the screen and locks onto the 4 wheels of the 2 cars, then he fires at the wheels, which makes the 2 cars fly up and flip sideways at the same time. He then drives up and overtakes 2 other cars. He releases spikes from behind his rear bumper, which pops the wheels of the 2 cars behind him. The Black Devil then overtakes another car and starts to speed up in front of it. The other car begins speeding and chasing the Black Devil from behind. The Black Devil starts to speed up even more; he then quickly slams on the brakes, which makes the speeding car from behind crash really hard into the back of the Black Devil's hovering car. Then from inside of the Black Devil's car the Black Devil puts his car on autopilot and presses a red button on his control panel which makes his chair shift to the middle of the car , and the empty passenger side chair goes back and folds underneath. The steering wheel changes and a shooting system plus a screen and controls come up. The Black Devil then grabs the firing sticks and starts shooting rockets and heavy bullets at the remaining vehicles in front of him. He starts to shoot them from behind, then the cars begin to flip over frontwards and crash. After shooting for a while the Black Devil manages to destroy nearly all the cars in front of him. He then makes his chair return to normal and he turns the autopilot off. Seconds later army jets and helicopters with rocket attachments come flying towards the Black Devil and the remaining cars. The military jets and helicopters then start to fire heavy artillery and rockets. After seeing this, the Black Devil and the remaining cars go off road and drive into the dark, ragged western terrain with cactuses.

The Black Devil contacts the Central City mayor and says, "Mayor, there's been a big misunderstanding. The army thinks I'm one of Black Skull's men. You need to contact the military and tell them I'm one of the good guys." Out of fear the Black Devil then starts speeding to the maximum of his capability. Within moments the remaining cars get taken out by rockets and heavy fire, then all the fire focuses on the Black Devil. The military starts firing rockets and bullets at the Black Devil's car. The Black Devil begins to scream; he speeds up and starts moving from side to side to avoid getting hit while the military fires rockets downwards. The ground begins to blow up just inches away from the Black Devil's car. The Black Devil then turns off all the lights on his car, slams on his brakes and moves backwards into the darkness. He disappears and the military quickly loses sight of him. Inside the shadows the Black Devil quickly puts his hovering car on autopilot. He then presses the detachment button and His bike begins to separate and come out from the side of the car (the steering side of the Black Devil's car can separate and become a bike). In the darkness he separates his bike from his car and rides his bike with the lights off to the side of the terrain. He then turns all the lights in his car on and starts making his hovering car move forward via remote control. The army sees the Black Devil's hovering car coming out of the darkness and they start following it. Because the lights are on and the military thinks the Black Devil is still inside driving, so they keep on following the brightly lit car until they can barely be seen. Then out of the darkness you hear a motorbike revving, the lights of the Black Devil's bike come on, and the Black Devil drives away, unharmed and undetected.

While all of the commotion is going on, the Black Skull and his men head for a different military base. The men he sent to rob the eastern military base were only a distraction so he can rob the western military base. The 2 commanders of the western military base are close friends of Black Skull, and they are also secret members of the League of Desolation.

The 2 commanders on that day gathered all the workers of the military base and asked them to come to the meeting room for an important announcement. All the workers come to the meeting room, and at the door they hand their guns over to 2 corrupt security guards. While one commander is giving the fake announcement the other commander turns off all the security cameras, he then opens the doors and allows the Black Skull and his men to come in. Black Skull and his men all come in silently, wearing gas masks and wielding pistols with silencer attachments. Then the Black Skull and his men all rush into the meeting room where all the military workers are seated, and they begin throwing sleeping and gas bombs onto the floor the gas engulfs the room and weakens all the soldiers inside. Then Black Skull and his men begin shooting and killing all the soldiers with their silent pistols.

After the massacre the two commanders get tied up by Black Skull's men so police would not suspect a thing after they arrive to the crime scene. The Black Skull and his men then take 100 grenade launchers and many weapons, including guns, bombs and grenades. After the police show up the 2 commanders lie and act like they had nothing to do with the incident. (The Black Skull wanted to accomplish 2 things: first he wanted to weaken and kill many soldiers so the military would be much weaker and much fewer in number once the civil war starts. And second, the Black Skull wanted to waste and steal a lot of the military's weapons, so when the war starts the military wouldn't have as many weapons to defend themselves with, making them much weaker and easier to defeat.)

After stealing the weapons from the military base the Black Skull secretly gives out weapons to nearly all the people who have joined the League of Desolation by calling them to come to many remote areas where most of the weapons are located and stored.

Chapter 20: Civil war

Black Skull shows up on national TV again and proclaims a final war, an all-out attack against Central City and America. He tells the people that he recruited, "Whoever has joined the League of Desolation and whoever has received his weapons, let him come and fight. The time has come to rise from the shadows and fight till you can't fight anymore, and whoever wants to stand against the corruption of the government, then let him stand with us and join the League of Desolation, the civil war starts now."

The new American government then has secret meeting, where they decide to send out hundreds of troops and police to the streets in order to quickly stop the civil war from escalating, and also to capture Black Skull, Quick Shot and the rest of their men.

Hours later all the civilians who have joined the League of Desolation come out to the streets, wielding high-class weapons. Then the American army comes and all hell breaks loose. The civilians and the American army begin to have an all-out civil war on the streets of Central City and across America. Many shops get broken into and cars get lit up on fire.

Meanwhile Black Skull sends a hundred men, all wielding rocket launchers, to take hostages. He commands half of his men to go and stand on Central City's rooftops. The other half are told to go stand next to the windows in high rise buildings. Black Skull grabs the Black Devil's wife and the Central City mayor and heads towards Central City tower with many armed men. At the Central City tower, the Black Skull and his men take everyone in Central City Tower as hostages. They tie them up and place them all on the 14th floor. Then the Black Skull and his men booby-trap the doors, fill the building with explosives, grab their guns and prepare for the police's coming. The police are gathered, the SWAT teams come to help and the police helicopters are ordered to shoot down all the men with rocket launchers. The Black Devil finds out about the situation and calls the Blue Eagle, then they both head to the battle scene. The Black Devil drives his new hovering devil car and the Blue Eagle flies the Black Devil's warplane. On the street, the war continues between the civilians and the military.

Meanwhile, Black Skull's men and Quick Shot are in a van parked right next to the White House. Two of the men inside the van hack through the White House's security systems and disable all of the White House's security cameras and replace them with still images rather than video. Then the men slowly get out, fully dressed like the Secret Service agents, wielding silent pistols. They then quietly take out the 6 real Secret Service agent guards standing at the front. They then put their bodies in the bushes and proceed to enter the White House. Along the way they silently kill a few other Secret Service agents, they then quickly enter the camera security room. The workers in the room are unaware of Quick Shot and Black Skull's men because the cameras are on still image mode, which makes everything seem normal. Quick Shot and his men enter the security room and take out the security workers, they then rush to the president's office and tell him, "Sir, there has been a breach. Your life is in danger; we must evacuate immediately." The president goes with them because he thinks they're the real Secret Service agents that have been sent to save him, not knowing that they're actually Quick Shot and his men dressed in fake Secret Service outfits.

Meanwhile, Black Skull gives the orders and his men from above start firing rockets at the American army below, blowing up many tanks, vehicles, and planes and killing hundreds of soldiers. The newly-recruited League of Desolation members witness the chaos and quickly take advantage of the situation. Thousands of men start rushing up and shooting the weakened army. They kill hundreds of soldiers, gain ground and begin slowly winning the war.

Meanwhile the Blue Eagle is flying in his aircraft; he puts his plane on autopilot and opens the window, comes out and stands on top of the aircraft while it's flying. He attaches a harness which prevents him from falling, he then starts sniping Black Skull's men. The police helicopters do the same: one cop drives and another cop stands next to the helicopter door sniping Black Skull's men.

The Black Devil comes driving to Central City tower, then he runs and attaches his shoes to the building located directly beside Central City tower. His shoes turn blue from underneath, and he starts running upwards on the building. He continues running up the high rise building until he almost reaches the top, but seconds before reaching the roof top the Black Devil gets hit with a massive rocket head, which makes the side of the building crumble and causes the Black Devil to fall straight down into a TNT explosives truck, the truck explodes and injures the Black Devil badly, then out of the wreckage and blazing dark fire the Black Devil emerges, fully transformed into the red Horned Devil. He flies up and screams loudly in anger. He then rushes towards and starts attacking all of Black Skull's men, who are located in the nearby streets and in all the nearby buildings. The transformed Black Devil starts attacking and blowing fire onto his enemies until he manages to kill 70% of Black Skull's men who were fighting on the nearby streets, and he also manages to kill 50 out of the one hundred men who were hiding inside the nearby buildings firing rocket launchers. And Because of the Black Devil's contribution the army once again gains the upper hand and starts advancing in the civil war.

But eventually the transformed Devil heads back to the streets and the effects of the devil serum wear off, and he transforms back into the Black Devil. He then heads back to Central City tower, and this time he climbs another nearby building and makes it all the way to the top (note: once the Black Devil transforms into the Red Devil he cannot transform again for at least 24 hours, and that was the Black Skull's plan exactly; the person who hit and injured the Black Devil with the rocket launcher was none other than the Black Skull. The Black Skull knew that if he managed to horribly injure the Black Devil he would transform and after his transformation ended, he would become weaker and he wouldn't be able to transform again for at least 24 hours; thus, the Black Skull would be able to defeat or kill the Black Devil. In his normal Black Devil form the Black Devil is beatable but when he transforms he becomes almost impossible to kill. Now Black Skull stands a big chance, and the fight is even and fair. The Black Skull's plan worked perfectly.)

Meanwhile, the SWAT team also gets on top of a nearby building which is located right next to Central City tower, then the SWAT team starts firing zip lines into the 15th floor of Central City tower they then start zip lining into the tower. Black Skull's men see the SWAT team coming and begin to cut the SWAT team's zip lines with bulk cutters, which makes many of the SWAT team fall to their deaths. However, about 21 SWAT team members manage to zip line and enter the tower from all sides. One of Black Skull's men screams, "SIR, WE'VE GOT COMPANY. MANY SWAT TEAM MEMBERS HAVE MANAGED TO ENTER THE 15th floor. We really need your help, sir."

The Black Skull quickly jumps down to the 15th floor and tells his men in a loud voice, "TAKE COVER." Then the SWAT team begin to fire bullets at Black Skull. The Black Skull quickly dodges the bullets, rushes up, attacks and breaks the necks of 3 SWAT team members, he then brings out two golden AK-47s from his back and starts laughing and firing at the remaining SWAT team members. Black Skull's men do the same and start shooting at the remaining SWAT team members from behind cover. Ten SWAT team members get shot and drop to the ground; the other 8 remaining SWAT team members take cover behind the concrete columns and walls and start firing back at Black Skull and his men.

The Black Skull starts moving side to side dodging the bullets, then the 6 remaining Swat team members rush up and start attacking the Black Skull. The Black Skull starts evading and dodging all their attacks with superhuman speed and agility, he then grabs one of them by the neck and launches him across the room and into the wall, the Black Skull then quickly does a spinning low kick on another SWAT team member. The SWAT team member trips and starts falling backwards but just seconds before hitting the ground the Black Skull quickly punches him hard to the face, breaks his jaw and launches him across the room, through the glass and out of the building .

The Black Skull then jumps up and does a super-fast 360-degree spinning kick. The kick lands and knocks another SWAT team member into the ground, then the 2 remaining nearby SWAT team members rush up and start firing at the Black Skull. The Black Skull

gets shot many times but doesn't get injured, then 2 SWAT team members rush up and start attacking the Black Skull at the same time. The Black Skull starts blocking and dodging all their kicks and punches and he starts countering and attacking back, then one of the SWAT team members throws a high kick. The Black Skull grabs it, picks him up and slams him right through the concrete floor, then he turns to the other SWAT team member and starts punching and kicking him with over

25 high-speed attacks. The SWAT team member becomes bruised all over his body and starts bleeding. The Black Skull then spins and kicks him to the chest. The SWAT team member flies back, breaks through the concrete wall and dies.

Now there are only 2 SWAT team members left and they're hiding behind the walls. The Blacks Skull tells them in a loud voice, "Come out, it's time to die." The 2 SWAT team members become terrified and start shooting at the Black Skull. They fire 50 shots but the Black Skull quickly dodges and grabs all the bullets. Then Black Skull's men gather around Black Skull, and the Black Skull says in a loud voice,

"I SENTENCE YOU AND YOUR GOVERMENTS TO EXECUTION--FIREEEEEEEEEEEE."

Then the Black Skull and all his men quickly point their guns towards the 2 remaining SWAT team members hiding behind the concrete walls and start firing hundreds upon hundreds of rounds of bullets towards the 2 SWAT team members. The hundreds of bullets penetrate the concrete walls and viciously kills the last 2 remaining SWAT team members. Black Skull then tells his men, "If anyone else tries to come in, kill them quickly, before they enter the building." He walks away and heads back upstairs to the 16th floor.

Meanwhile, downstairs the military is on the ground and they're trying to safely get into the tower from the front and back doors. They open the doors and get blown away because the doors of Central City tower were booby-trapped with explosives, but the other remaining soldiers rush into the tower and start firing at Black Skull's men. Black Skull's men begin to fire back, and as the war is going on inside Central City tower the Black Devil is still standing on top of the building. He then pulls out a gun that, when fired, releases smoke bombs which put's people to sleep. He fires 10 rounds of smoke bombs into the 15th floor (Black Skull is on the 16th floor). On the 15th floor smoke begins to fill the room, and Black Skull's men begin to feel its effect. They become tired and weak. The Black Devil then quickly glides into the 15th floor, breaks through the glass and begins attacking Black Skull's men. Black Skull's men try to fight back, but the Black Devil throws a tiny round bomb which rapidly releases 20 tiny needles. When these needles penetrate the skin people quickly go to sleep. The needles penetrate and put most of the men to sleep. The other men slowly approach the Black Devil, but the Black Devil easily knocks them all out, he then proceeds to the 16th floor. There he finds Black Skull, 5 guards, his wife and the mayor sitting on the ground with guns pointed at their heads.

Black Skull looks at the Black Devil and says, "OH, IF IT ISN'T THE COWBOY, JONATHON KLYDE. I had a feeling you would make it. Soon Quick Shot and my men will be kidnapping the president from the White House, hijacking his plane and then driving it straight through Central City tower with him in it. We will frame the president, then we will take over this country. Your precious president is about to die. The president will fall and then the League of Desolation will rise from the ashes and we will finally reclaim our rightful positions as leaders of a new world. But before the plane hits, one of my men will be picking me up from the roof top with a helicopter."

The Black Devil replies, "That won't be happening. I'm going to kill you right here, right now."

Black Skull says, "Can't you see, Jonathon, this has been my destiny all along? To become leader of this corrupt country and to destroy you, your family and everything you and your father have ever worked for."

The Black Devil calls up the Blue Eagle and tells him, "Blue Eagle, Quick Shot and his men are about to kidnap the president and drive his private jet straight into Central City tower. You must stop them now; there's no time."

The Blue Eagle hears the message. He puts his plane on autopilot , jumps off his plane and starts flying extremely fast towards the White House. Along the way the Blue Eagle dodges many bullets and heavy fire and he starts snatching and throwing many of Black Skull's men onto cars and other objects in order to knock them out, so they will stop shooting and killing the army and innocent civilians.

The Black Skull then says, "So now tell me, which member should we kill first? You choose--will it be your beloved wife Malisa Klyde or will it be the great mayor of Central City?"

The Black Devil replies, "John, you don't have to do this. There are things you just don't understand. Your father was a criminal. He killed my family. Yes, I did kill him, but I had no choice; his reign of terror had to come to an end."

The Black Skull says, "Everyone has a choice, Jonathon; there's no need for your lies. What gives you the right to take the lives of my family and friends? You and this city have been nothing but trouble. My mother was murdered in this city by a criminal, which led to my father being a criminal. My father lost his mind. We were living on the streets; while the rich sat back in comfort and did nothing to help us, we the poor people were living in darkness and misery. The rich ate while we starved, and when a good man named Razor came to change the state of this city, the so-called hero of Central City brutally killed him. You claim you're the good guy, Central City's so-called hero, yet you kill the innocent." The Black Devil's wife then says, "Whatever happens, honey, know that I love you and I'll always be with you."

The Black Skull gives the order and 2 guards rush up and grab the Black Devil tightly by his arms. Black Skull shouts, "KILL THEM, KILL THEM ALL." Then Jonathon Klyde's wife and the mayor get shot in front of the Black Devil's eyes. The Black Devil gets really angry and kills the 2 guards holding him. The other 3 guards rush up and start attacking the Black Devil but the Black Devil quickly and easily kills all three of them.

Then the Black Skull points the automatic gun towards the Black Devil, then throws it out the window and says, "I'll kill you with my own two hands." The Black Devil rushes up, then the Black Skull and the Black Devil start fighting.

While Black Skull and the Black Devil are fighting, Quick Shot and his men get into the private jet with the president inside. They grab the president and handcuff him to the chair of the plane's cockpit.

The president says, "What's the meaning of this? You are breaking international law. You're the Secret Service and you've been sent by the UN to protect me. Don't you know who I am? I'm the President of the United States." Quick Shot then takes off his fake facial hair, puts on his costume and mask and tells the president, "Well, Mr. President, we are your worst nightmare. The League of Desolation are here to take over."

Before the jet can take off, the Blue Eagle quickly flies in through the narrow gap of the plane's door. Quick Shot turns to the Blue Eagle and says, "Ooh, so you're the infamous Blue Eagle, the Black Devil's right-hand man. We have heard so much about you, like how you glide through Central City's rooftops and sky protecting the innocent and striking down the criminals and the corrupt. We can use someone of your caliber. I will give you 2 choices: either join us now or die where you stand."

The Blue Eagle replies, "You and the rest of your organization are insane. You have destroyed our city and killed our people. I will never join you; rather, I will be the one who stops you."

Quick Shot gets angry, pulls out a gun and starts shooting at the Blue Eagle but the Blue Eagle runs and takes cover behind the plane's doors and furniture. Then three of Quick Shot's men run towards the airplane's cockpit and hack the jet's controls and autopilot the plane straight for Central City tower. Quick Shot's men then give the president a cell phone and a piece of paper with writing on it, they then put a gun towards the president's shoulders and tell him in a loud voice, "You are going to call up the news station and read what is written on this paper to them, then the news stations are going to record it and publish it all across the country. If you refuse to do what we say, you will be dealt with very harshly."

The president says, "Ok, I will do whatever you want but please don't harm me." The president starts shaking, he then calls up the main news channel in America and starts reading what's on the paper. The word quickly spreads and all the newsrooms and radios around the entire country pick up on the president's recorded phone call. The phone call starts airing on all the media and TV stations live. The people gather around their TVs and radios to hear what the president is saying, then the president says, "My fellow Americans, this is your newly-elected president speaking. Please listen to me carefully because I have something really important to say. Since the extermination and fall of the previous government called the Rebels, you the people elected us, the Republican Party of America, to take their place in order to fix all the problems and make this great country a much better place for all its people, but I'm afraid we have not done that. We are just as bad as the previous U.S. government who called themselves the League of Rebellion in secret.

"For over 5 years now we the new Republican party of America have been lying to all of you people. We have been stealing from you and causing corruption, misery and poverty across America, and right now I'm inside my private jet and I'm about to crash this jet straight into Central City tower, causing millions of dollars in damages. If you truly want to follow a righteous government, then I recommend you follow the League of Desolation. The League of Desolation are honest men who fight for the freedom and liberation of all Americans."

As the president is reading the forced fake speech we hear his voice in the background, and we start seeing slow motion scenes of the civil war across the country, we see recruited civilians shooting the army and the army shooting back and killing the recruited civilians, and in other parts of town we see crooks breaking into shops, stealing all their merchandise and then setting the shops on fire, and other thugs terrorizing defenseless people and breaking, stealing and setting cars and city property on fire. As the civil war and chaos continues the president keeps on reading.

"The League of Desolation fight to bring the newly-elected American government down, and who could blame them? We the new Republican party of America are truly an evil and corrupt government, so join and support the League of Desolation, because they truly care about the people, and they will do anything for your freedom and protection."

Straight after the president finishes his forced fake speech Quick Shot's men turn the cell phone off, they then grab the president's forearm and inject him with a sleeping syringe. The president fall's asleep and Quick Shot's men leave and head for the plane door.

Meanwhile the Blue Eagle and Quick Shot are still fighting inside the plane. One of Quick Shot's men calls up Black Skull and gives him a message saying, "Boss, we have put the president to sleep. You need to get out of Central City tower right now. The private jet will be hitting the tower in exactly 15 minutes. A helicopter is waiting for you on the rooftop." After hearing this Black Skull says to the Black Devil, "The plane will collide in 15 minutes, and fifteen minutes is more than enough time for me to kill you and escape with my life." They then proceed to have the most epic fight ever seen.

Meanwhile Quick Shot and the Blue Eagle are fighting inside the private plane. One of Black Skull's men inside the plane tells Quick Shot in a loud panicked voice, "QUICK SHOT, WE HAVE TO LEAVE NOW. THIS PLANE IS GOING TO CRASH. WE WILL ALL DIE."

Then Quick Shot replies in a loud, angry voice, "IF YOU WANT TO LEAVE THEN BE MY GUEST, BUT I'M NOT LEAVING THIS PLANE UNTIL I KILL THIS MAN." Quick Shot's men know they will never be able to convince Quick Shot, so they decide to leave without him. They open the plane door; they then jump out and open their parachutes. Quick Shot then looks around the plane and finding that the Blue Eagle has disappeared, he suddenly rushes to the plane door. The Blue Eagle then drops from the ceiling, grabs his metal pole, and hits Quick Shot upwards on his hands, which in turn makes

Quick Shot's guns fly out of the plane door and into the open air. The Blue Eagle smiles and says, "Now you have no chance; without your guns you're nothing."

Quick Shot replies, "We will see about that. You're nothing but a dead man." Quick Shot pulls out his sword and the Blue Eagle grabs his blue electricity metal pole and they proceed to fight. During the fight the Blue Eagle breaks and knocks the sword out of Quick Shot's hand, Quick Shot gets angry rushes up and starts punching and kicking the Blue Eagle. The Blue Eagle blocks some of Quick Shot's attacks, but others land hard. The hard shots stun the Blue Eagle. Quick Shot takes this opportunity, grabs the Blue Eagle and starts throwing and slamming him around the planes furniture and walls. Quick Shot then lets him go and the Blue Eagle falls and collapses on the ground. Quick Shot then picks him up again and throws him into the plane's cupboard. The cupboard breaks and a huge modern and powerful black automatic gun falls out and lands on presidential table.

Both the Blue Eagle and Quick Shot see the modern powerful gun, and they both know whoever grabs the gun first will be able to kill the other. Quick Shot runs towards the table so he can grab the gun, but the Blue Eagle quickly jumps on the table and kicks the gun away backwards before Quick Shot could grab it. Quick Shot then jumps on the table, and both of them proceed to have an epic fight on the presidential table, but in the end the Blue Eagle throws a hard spinning back kick to Quick Shot's face, which makes Quick Shot fall off the table and hit the ground hard. Then the Blue Eagle does a back flip off the table and lands next to the black gun. The Blue

Eagle quickly grabs the black automatic gun and aims it towards Quick Shot. Quick Shot becomes terrified and in total desperation he runs towards the Blue Eagle in order to stop him from shooting, but seconds before Quick Shot could reach him, the Blue Eagle unloads and fires the automatic gun. The endless barrage of powerful bullets begins to push Quick Shot backwards. The Blue Eagle keeps on firing and pushing Quick Shot back until the Blue Eagle runs out of bullets and Quick Shot reaches the very end of the plane door. The Blue Eagle then quickly flies towards Quick Shot, grabs him, and launches him out of the plane door. Now Quick Shot is freefalling to his death, so the Blue Eagle keeps hitting him in the air and just seconds before impact, the Blue Eagle pushes off and kicks Quick Shot with both of his legs. Quick Shot slams on the ground and dies, while the Blue Eagle flies up and travels to safety.

The Blue Eagle then quickly rushes back to the private jet. He enters the plane door and heads to the plane's controls and tries to un-hack them, but he fails to do so. He then calls the Black Devil and tells him, "Hey Black Devil, you really need to get out of that tower. The controls are jammed and this plane is about to crash straight into Central City tower." Then the Blue Eagle looks at the president's body and says, "I'm going to get you out of here, Mr. President." The Blue Eagle unties the president and carries him on his shoulders, he then grabs the black automatic gun and starts shooting holes into the plane's metal floor. The floor collapses and the Blue Eagle falls straight down, into "the devil's war plane." The Blue Eagle directed the plane to come under the jet with his hand watch (the Blue Eagle can't shoot the private jet down by using the "devil's plane's" rockets simply because if he does it will come crashing into the city below, killing hundreds of innocent people).

Meanwhile, Black Skull and the Black Devil continue their fight while the plane rapidly moves closer. The Black Skull becomes more violent and gets the upper hand; he grabs the Black Devil, locks his arms and brings him to his knees. He then grabs a powerful automatic gun from his back pocket and points it at the Black Devil 's head, and says, "This is for my father." The Black Devil has a flashback of his mother and his family getting shot. A tear comes to his eye, and he gets angry like never before. The Black Devil then turns around, grabs the gun and moves it away from his face. He then gets up, takes the Black Skull's gun and starts firing bullets at the Black Skull. The Black Skull begins to catch and avoid all the bullets, then the Black Skull laughs and say's, "Is that all you've got? Well, now it's my turn--let me show you what I can do. Prepare to witness the legendary art of superhuman capoeira."

The Black Skull rushes up, jumps and does a super-fast 360-degree spinning kick. The kick lands and hits the Black Devil in the face, the Black Skull then rushes up again. The Black Devil sees him coming. They come face to face and the Black Devil starts throwing many powerful kicks and punches, but the Black Skull easily starts blocking dodging and counterattacking all the Black Devil's kicks and punches. The Black Devil then tries again. This time he throws a wild haymaker but the

Black Skull sees the punch coming and ducks the attack. The Black Skull then quickly jumps up, spins and hits the Black Devil with a spinning back kick to his face. The powerful kick lands and launches the Black Devil backwards into the hard concrete pillar, then the Black Skull quickly follows up with a spinning back kick to the stomach, which makes the Black Devil go straight through the pillar, breaking the concrete in half. The Black Devil screams and drops to the ground; the Black Skull then picks him up by his neck and throws him across the room into another concrete pillar. The pillar once again breaks in half and crumbles.

The Black Skull says in an angry voice, "Can you feel the pain you caused me? Good. Well, now it's time to feel some more."

The Black Skull runs towards the Black Devil, the black devil then quickly grabs a time bomb and throws it in the air. Everything becomes slow motion, then the Black Devil grabs 2 glowing energy fuses from his belt and places them inside his glove compartment. His right glove starts glowing red and his left glove starts glowing blue. The effects of the time bomb wear off, everything returns to normal, and the Black Skull says, "What just happened?"

The Black Devil looks at Black Skull and says in a loud, angry voice, "DODGE THIS." the Black Devil then fires red and blue energy sparks from his gloves. The thousands of blue and red sparks engulf the entire room and head towards the Black Skull like a barrage of sparkling neon bullets. The Black Skull tries to dodge the blasts but he fails to do so. Nearly all the blasts hit him directly and injure him badly, knocking him back into the wall. The Black Skull becomes angry, gets up and they continue on fighting. During the fight The Black Skull once again ends up winning most of the exchanges, and injures the black devil, the Black Devil becomes extremely angry. The power of the devil serum ignites his body, and he becomes faster and more powerful. The Black Skull begins to attack the Black Devil with everything he's got but the Black Devil manages to block and counterattack nearly all of the Black Skull's attacks. The Black Devil then starts attacking and hitting the Black Skull with many powerful punches and kicks. The Black Skull then panics' and throws a powerful punch, the Black Devil grabs the Black Skull's arm and breaks it in half. The Black Skull then screams and says, "Ahh, ahh, what have you done? You will pay for that."

The Black Skull then rushes up and kicks the Black Devil in the head. The Black Devil dodges the kick and hits the Black Skull with a hard elbow straight to the chin and follows up with five heavy haymakers, and ten jabs and uppercuts to the face. The Black Skull gets rocked and in total desperation he throws a final punch. The Black Devil blocks it, then kicks him really hard to the chest; straight after the kick the Black Skull stumbles backwards towards the windows. The Black Devil then sees and grabs a grenade bomb from the ground and throws it near the Black Skull's face. The bomb explodes and injures the Black Skull badly. The Black Skull stumbles back and hits the large glass windows hard. The glass windows begin to break and crack slowly the Black Devil then quickly rushes up jumps and kicks the Black Skull straight to the face. The glass window breaks, and the Black Skull falls out of the window and hits the concrete street below then dies.

The Black Devil takes a last look at the Black Skull. He then turns around and says his final goodbyes to the dead bodies of his wife and the mayor of Central City. He then looks at the main window and sees the president's huge private jet coming straight at the building at full speed. He panics and begins to run in the opposite direction as fast as he can towards the back windows. The plane hits the building, and the fire and the wreckage from the building and the plane starts heading towards the Black Devil. The Black Devil becomes terrified and starts running even faster, then he quickly jumps out of the back window, breaks the glass and glides to safety. Seconds later , the Central City tower blows up and crashes to the ground.

In the end the Black Devil survives and nearly all of Black Skull's thugs get arrested. Central City begins reconstruction and a memorial service is held to remember Jonathon Klyde's wife, the mayor and all who have died. An investigation clears the president's name and the newly-elected Republican party of America regains the people's trust and support back once again. The president honors the Blue Eagle with a medal and drops all his charges.

Eight years later, the Black Devil is in his cattle ranch home spending time with his son when he suddenly sees a scary vision of a large beast standing in front of him and saying, "You think you're safe. I will kill you. You will not be able to help them; you're nothing to me, all your training and all youre heroic work will not save you from me; your world and the devil realm belong to infernoooooooo." Then Jonathon Klyde pops back to reality and hears a knock on his door. The Black Devil and his son answer the door and see a good devil they have never met before, who tells them, "The greatest battle between good and evil is about to begin. Please prepare yourselves and come with me."

The end

Paperback ISBN: 9780994484208

For any business inquiries or feedback please contact me by email or contact number:
Name: Ossama Quiader
My email: quiader22@yahoo.com.au
Home phone: 02 97085717
Mobile phone: 0406 012 625
I live in Sydney, Australia.

If you enjoyed this book and its content then please give it a good review online, that would be greatly appreciated, thank you.

Pictures of : Ossama Quiader the author of this book shown down below